# THE KISSING

*a collection of short stories*

## MERLINDA BOBIS

D1601162

*aunt lute books*
*San Francisco*

First Edition

10 9 8 7 6 5 4 3 2 1

Aunt Lute Books
P.O. Box 410687
San Francisco, CA 94141

Cover Art: "Heliconia" Copyright ©1995 by Pacita Abad
Cover Design by Kajun Design

Senior Editor: Joan Pinkvoss
Managing Editor: Shay Brawn

Production: Gina Gemello, Shahara Godfrey, Laura Reizman,
Golda Sargento

This collection first published in 1999 by Spinifex Press Pty Ltd,
North Melbourne, Australia.

This book was funded in part by grants from the California Arts
Council, the National Endowment for the Arts, the Australia Council
for the Arts, and the San Francisco Arts Commission Cultural Equity
Program.

Library of Congress Cataloging-in-Publication Data

Bobis, Merlinda C. (Merlinda Carullo)
    The kissing : a collection of short stories / Merlinda Bobis.—1st ed.
    p. cm.
    ISBN 1-879960-60-5
        1. Philippines—Social life and customs—Fiction. 2. Australia—
    Social life and customs—Fiction. I. Title.

PR9550.9.B58 K57 2001
823'.914—dc21

                                                        2001022720

*For Mama, Papa,*
*Mama Ola*
*and John*

# ACKNOWLEDGEMENTS

A number of these stories were originally published in *Australian Short Stories*, *Heat*, *Hecate*, *Philippine Free Press*, *Philippine Graphic*, *Picador New Writing 4* and *Southerly*.

"An Earnest Parable" was broadcast by ABC Radio National as one of the winners of its 1997 Books and Writing Short Story Competition; "White Turtle" has also won the 1998 Ashes Trans-Tasman Short Story Competition.

# TABLE OF CONTENTS

# AN EARNEST PARABLE

As it was his turn that day to lose his tongue, he had for breakfast the creamiest *latik*, a dish of sticky rice in coconut milk, served with a large, ripe mango. Then he sang two serenades about love and volcanoes in the Philippines. He was making the most of his chance for taste and speech, because, an hour later, his Sri Lankan neighbour would be at the door, awaiting her turn. Already, she would be dreaming of pappadums and hot curries, not quite as spicy as her dialect which would melt on the much-awaited tongue. Their communal tongue.

Bessel Street's most precious possession. Last week, it lodged with the Italian butcher who earlier had picked it up from the Australian couple. The butcher was not one to waste time. Immediately, he laid this soft, pink flesh, moist with the previous owner's steak and peppercorns, inside his mouth. Then he ran to the mirror with his wife and three daughters and began savouring his first words after weeks of silence: "*bellisima, bellisima!*" The whole family marvelled at how, like a pink animal, the tongue rolled its tip to the roof of the mouth in an intimate curl – "*bellllllll–isima* . . ." Then they passed the tongue around, taking turns to relish old, native sounds, after which they dined on home-made pasta in a piquant marinara sauce.

The residents of Bessel Street were kin in tongue. The pink flesh toured up and down that street, went into homes, into mouths of different origins. There was the baker from Turkey, the Filipino cook, the Australian couple with the fish shop, the Italian butcher and the Sri Lankan tailor.

One tongue for five homes. Not really an inconvenient arrangement, mind you. Of course, when the tongue was accommodated elsewhere, one could not eat with the usual joys of the palate. But the pleasure of the ear was enough compensation. Every tongue-owner's soundings, especially those that were heard as foreign noises, seemed to orchestrate in everyone else's middle ear into something intimate and comforting. This was inevitable for, muted at different times, they learned how to listen intently to whoever had the chance for speech or song – and how they spoke and sang and even told stories, usually with words of beauty and kindness. The moment of speech was too dear to be wasted on loose, heart-less talk. It was a shame not to do justice to the little, pink animal in the mouth.

Thus everyone spoke, ate and listened with care and passion, and shared various languages and delicacies. Last week, for instance, the word "*bella*" found its way into a Turkish ditty whose refrain would later inspire the new name of the Australian fish shop, which supplied the mussels for the butcher's marinara that sneaked into the Filipino chef's kitchen, where it was blessed – *Dios mabalos!* – as an afterthought, with a dollop of coconut cream and some red chillies, well, to give it teeth, the Sri Lankan tailor reckoned, before the dish was resurrected among the *pides* of the Turkish baker.

Indeed, on their respective days of owning the tongue, each of the neighbours could not help but echo the mouth of the previous owner. The Italian family eventually developed a taste for the occasional cardamom tea, the Filipino adventurously spread some Vegemite on his *pan de sal* and, at one time, the Australian couple stirred fish heads into their sour soup. Meanwhile, the Sri Lankan began hosting summer feasts by the barbie, and the Turkish baker even serenaded his wife with songs about love and volcanoes as he prepared a tray of almond *biscotti* for the oven.

You see, the tongue had an excellent memory. Even when it had moved to a new mouth, it still evoked the breath of spices, sweets and syllables of the former host. It was never known to forget anything, least of all the fact that it was once the soft, pink flesh of a South Coast mollusc; it yielded itself to a higher good one winter night when the ocean was formidably wild. The six households understood this origin in their mouths. The tongue was a gift of the landscape. The *pides* and *gulab jamuns*, the daily *buongiornos* and even the highly spiced curries and love serenades could never drown the unmistakable tang of Australian surf and grit – and, truly like surf, after this home truth was dramatised on TV's latest culinary show, the heart of one viewing nation swelled and swelled with pride.

# FRUIT STALL

I am forty. Divorced. No children. I own a fruit stall in Kings Cross. And I am Filipina, but this is my secret. People ask, are you Spanish? Mexican? Italian? A big man, brushing his hairy arm against my waist, whispers in his beer-breath, aha, *Latina*! Cringing, I say, *si, si, si* to him, and to all of them. I am Filipina, but this is my secret.

I dyed my hair brown. It goes well with this pale skin from my Spanish grandfather whom I never saw. He owned the *hacienda* where my grandmother served as housemaid. They sent her away when she grew a melon under her skirt.

Melons have their secret, too. No one knows how many seeds hide in their rose-flesh. Or who planted them there. Mother used to say, it is God, it is God who plants all things. I don't believe her now.

"Is this sweet?"

"Very sweet. And few seeds." I pretend to know a secret.

But he's not interested. This man frowning at the melon sounds like a customer back home. He touches the fruit doubtingly, tentatively. His hand is smooth and white against the green rind.

"Want a taste?" I offer the last slice from a box labelled "For Tasting". I pretend I am a fruitseller at home where we let the buyer sample the merchandise before any business takes place.

Sample the merchandise. This is how the men, who go to my country to find themselves a nice, little brown girl, put it. They're great, these rice-ies. Give them a bowl of rice and they can fuck all night! An American serviceman said this once, grabbing me by the waist. I was twelve then. I remember I went home crying.

He gets it cheaply. He walks away with the melon now, the man with the smooth, white hand. More like the hands of my grandfather. Mine are white, too, but hard and rough.

So father said, papayas are good for your skin. Mash them well with your hands tonight, so they get soft and smooth when Jake arrives. Remember to be nice to him, ha? And fix that face – *Dios mio*, will you stop snivelling? Jake, the old Australian whom my father had met in the city, became my husband. It must have been the papayas.

They're too small here and not as sweet. See these here? Too expensive, but not as good as the papayas back home. The tourists go gaga over our papayas there. They are sun-ripe, tree-ripe, we say. And cheap. Have dollar, no problem.

"How much for this?" Her hand on the papaya is very tanned, with fine golden hair. She's wearing a T-shirt with a coconut print. She looks happy. Good holiday. I want to ask, did you go to my country? But I keep my secret safe.

She frowns though, when I tell her the price. You see, papayas are expensive here. Go to my country. We sell them cheaply. I bite my tongue.

"And a kilo of grapes as well, please."

My youngest brother ate himself sick with the grapes which Jake brought from Australia to our village. It was the first time my brothers tasted grapes. It was the first time our neighbours tasted grapes. Jake was very pleased with himself. He promised more grapes. A week before the wedding, my father strutted about, imagining himself the father-in-law of a grape-king. When I came here, I found out grapes are very cheap, especially in late summer.

It was getting cold when I arrived. Autumn is cold for me. Winter is freezing. Hardly any grapes by then. Jake said we were too greedy – why are you always sending something home? He must have suspected I sneaked in some grapes in my letters. He opened them. He frowned at my dialect on paper. What stories are you telling them, huh?

I can tell many stories about sweaty white hands running all over me in front of other men nodding over their beer. Guess where she's from? Oh, no, I didn't get myself an Asian with small tits. This is no Asian. Look at her melons. And they taste like plums – don't they, luv? He laughed until he was beetroot-red, while his fingers fumbled at my buttons, much to the joy of his clapping and stamping mates. My ex-husband was a fruitseller. I learned my trade from him, and I learned to say, *si*, I am Spanish. Or, Mexican by birth, *Señorita*. Or, Italian, *Signore*.

He reminded me of the pet monkey we had when I was young. My father gave it away, because it would wake up the whole house in the middle of the night with its crazed monkey-sounds. Jake did the same, chattering away about his great big white banana getting bigger and harder – turn over. On your belly, quick. He was very quick. Then he snored his way through a land of fruit. I imagined it had an overripe smell that made me sick. After a while, I learned how to doze off dry-eyed and dream of fruit-flies tracking down the smell, feeding on the smell, until each one dropped dead from too much sweetness.

I keep my stall clean and insect free. White people are particular about what they put in their bellies. Don't get me wrong. I don't say this is bad. I only say they're lucky, they have the choice to be particular. That's why I like it here. Actually, I liked it more after the divorce papers were signed. Oh, yes, I love it now, I do not wish to go home any more. Who would want to see a divorced woman there anyway? My mother with her strange God? My grape-less father? Never mind. I can have more than grapes here. I also have mangoes, pineapples, avocadoes, even guavas around me. I smell home each day.

"*Kumusta.*"

The woman with the red headband must have smelled what I smell. She smiles with the greeting I know so well. The blond man beside her is smiling, too, at her expectant face.

"*Kumusta.*" She is in earnest.

He shifts his gaze at me.

"You mean, *como esta?*" I pretend to look confused. "Of course, of course – *muy bien.*"

"Told ya, yer wrong, hon." He strokes her hair.

"But –" she searches my unsmiling face – "you're not Filipina?"

"You're Filipina." I stare back.

"Yes, oh, yes," she nods vigorously. "Arrived two months ago with my husband here – your mangoes, very expensive –"

"From Queensland, that's why," I shrug.

"May I?" She lifts a mango and smells it hungrily.

"Geez, isn't she pretty?" The husband runs his fingers through her hair again. The red band gets caught in his large, white hand.

"This one, please." She lays the prized fruit on the weighing tray and quickly rearranges her band.

"Only one? Let's have a kilo – nah, two kilos, if you want, hon." He winks at me, before proceeding to stroke her hair again. "Ain't I lucky?"

"Where I lived, we have a yard of mangoes."

I go for mangoes, too. Jake said we were not only grape-starved, but mango-greedy as well. I told him I would be asking for green mangoes if I were back home. He didn't understand what I meant until I started having fainting spells. He took me to the doctor "to fix me up". He did not want brown kids. I never told anyone.

"Let me tell ya, the Filipino *kumusta* comes from the Spanish *como esta*. The Philippines was once under Spain, y'see," the husband lectures me on my ancestry.

"Spain very far . . ." Her sweeping gesture leaves an unfinished arc in the air. "A long way?"

"The other side of the world, honey." He brings her hand to her side, then draws her closer.

"Hard for you, yes – ?"

"One gets used to it – ten dollars for these, thanks."

As they turn to go, I notice the blowfly, a big black seed dotting the last slice of melon for tasting. Must have been here for ages! All because of that bloody chatter – I roll a newspaper and get a good grip. Ay, my knuckles have never looked so white.

# FISH-HAIR WOMAN

Lemon grass. When the river was sweet with its scent, they came for me. Half an hour after the Angelus, *kang nag-aagaw su diklom buda su liwanag* – when the dark was wrestling with the light, as we say – they came in a haze of the first fireflies. Tinsel on the green uniforms of the three men, bordering a sleeve here, circling a belt there, filling buttonholes, dotting an insignia, and smothering the mouth of the M16 slung over a sergeant's shoulder. He of the sullen face – young Ramon, wasn't it? So like a dark angel then with his halo of darting lights, harbinger of omens from the river. I'm sure it's lemon grass and, *putang ina*, too many fireflies, he said, swatting the light on his pouting lips. That night, the roots of my hair knew this was going to be the last time, the last time, and I heard keening in my scalp.

A river sweet with lemon grass and breathing fireflies – how could you believe such a tale? I did not want to believe either, but in our Iraya we had mastered the art of faith, because it was the only way to believe we existed, that our village was still alive somewhere in the south of Luzon during that purge by the military. So when they asked me to come with them to fish out the lemon grass scent and give them back the river, the one that is sweetened only by the hills, I believed, and believed too that, just then, every strand of my hair heard my heart break.

Hair. How was it linked with the heart? I'll tell you – it had something to do with memory. Every time I remembered anything that unsettled my heart, my hair grew at least one handspan. Mamay Dulce was convinced of this phenomenon when I was six years old. *Makarawon na buhok, makarawon na puso* – very tricky hair, very tricky heart, she used to whisper to me in her singsong on mornings when I woke up to even longer hair on my pillow after a night of agitated dreams. You had long dreams last night, child, with long memories, too, she would say.

But were you alive when the soldiers came, I could have affirmed our secret tall tale with more clarity. You see, Mamay, history hurts my hair, did you know that? Remembering is always a bleeding out of memory, like pulling thread from a vein in the heart, a coagulation so fine, miles of it stretching upwards to the scalp, then sprouting there into the longest strand of red hair. Some face-saving tale to explain my twelve metres of very thick black hair with its streaks of red and hide my history. I am a Filipina, tiny and dark as a coconut husk, but what red fires glint on my head! Red as the dahlia blooms on the hedge, the neighbouring kids used to whisper in awe a long time ago.

I was still as awesome that last night of my twenty-seventh year when the village believed everything, especially all the whisperings woven about me and my hair. It was after all their salvation or the salvation of their beloved river, where much of daily life flowed, including sanity. This they believed with such insane hope, the way they trusted in undying love, in martyrdom and resurrection, and, of course, in beatific visions that made every road a possible Damascus; thus their comfort in the fireflies and lemon grass of the river even on that fatal day. Ay, the arm of conversion grows longer and more absurd in a desperate hour. Even thousands of miles away from the road where San Pablo was overpowered by the light of love, because of our own military persecution at the time, our Iraya thought that the river fireflies were shards of that old light. Perhaps, it would not strike the soldiers, but would smother them instead, their mouths, eyes, guns, into dumbness or blindness, even into mercy. A conversion into something close to love. But, as I said, young Ramon only swatted the stray light on his forever pouting lips, then ordered me to get my hair ready for the river.

"Fish with your hair, woman." Always that command which summed up my life. After the government declared its total war against the rebels, I realised the purpose of my being, why I had come to be such a freak of nature, why I was more hair than body, the span of it nearly thrice my whole frame. What incredible length and thickness and strength. Not my beauty as one would usually boast of this crowning glory, but my scourge, which made me feel and look top heavy, as if anytime I would be dragged down by whirlpools of black with red lights and there get lost, never to be found again.

Where is she? Always the question which passed from lips to lips, all pursed between a knowing smile and worry or pain, much like the way a mouth contorts after the first sip of good fish soup with too much lemon in it. Where is she? Ay, washing her hair in the river, of course, or, drying it now, perhaps, combing it, braiding it – but where is she? With her hair, where else, all of Iraya chuckled. Where is she? Eating with her hair, sleeping with her hair, taking her hair for a wander.

But they would never say, cutting it. If anyone as much as whispered this disaster, the whole village would have been at my door, a desperate stampede of hearts arguing, weeping for their river's sake, for their lives' sake – for our Iraya, *kaheraki kami*. Hair of Estrella, have mercy on us. The only time when they would speak or even remember my name. Where is she? With her hair. Who is she? The Fish-Hair Woman. How little we know or wish to know of the history of our icons or our saints or our gods. It is enough that we invent for them a present and believe that they can save us from ourselves. But, no, I will not allow you to invent me, too, you who read this, so I will tell you everything. And if you need saving at all, understand that I had relinquished salvation after that last night by the river.

> *lambat na itom na itom*
> *pero sa dugo natumtom*
> *samong babaying parasira*
> *buhok pangsalbar-pangsira*
> *kang samong mga padaba*
> *hale sa salog . . .*

> very black net
> but blood-soaked
> our fisherwoman
> hair to save-fish
> all our beloved
> from the river . . .

. . . from the river. Sergeant Ramon mumbled the refrain of this local song to the first Australian in our Iraya, while pointing the M16 at him. It was three months before that night of lemon grass and fireflies, on another night when the rifles were silvered by the moon, when I met Tony McIntyre. Trouble-maker-researcher-cum-crazy-nosy-tourist-cum-bullshitting-novelist-in-search-for-material-is-why-he-is-here-he-says, Ramon babbled, a jealous quaver in his breathlessness. The Australian was caught spying on me as I unbraided my hair at the bank of the river, and there was a bit of a chase, an understatement by Tony who later told me that it felt like a scene from a 'Nam documentary. Among the limonsito and milflores, he thought he could vanish in a jungle of red berries and lilac blooms, his pink and white face hopefully blending with the tropical foliage, until he felt the cold nudge of steel on his nape – get up, you spying *Amerikano*! And Tony thought, thank god, I'm Australian, then stupidly broke into a run – but Ramon would never shoot anyone in front of me. Hello, I held out a hand to the ashen-faced stranger, and Ramon never forgave him.

But forgive me if I'm outrunning you who read this. This is how my hair remembers, always without restraint, quickly netting the past in a swirl of black with red fire. Such was the thought which occurred to me after the sullen boy-soldier ordered me to prepare for my final trek to the river.

"You're eating fireflies, Ramon." A strange voice, sorrow creeping at the edges. I realised it was mine.

Under my hut's window, his lips shimmered with the tinsel creatures of the night. "Quickly woman – and shut up!"

The two other men waited at the steps while their young sergeant charged up my stairs in a cloud of fireflies. "Pests, pests," he waved them away with the butt of his gun. "This is what he brought with him, pestilence. Can't you see now?"

"Fireflies and lemon grass never hurt anyone." My scalp ached so. Piled on my head, the braids of hair began to grow again. A chain of handspans, too much remembering.

Enough, enough, I wanted to scream at this phosphorescent boy whose face was contorted with jealousy.

"The river is not fit for drinking again, don't you know that? Lemon grass taste, bah! And the light from these flies, *putang ina*! They've scared all the fishes away!" His grip on my arm bordered on an urgent caress as he thrust his tortured face to mine. "All because you fucked him!"

Tony McIntyre, my lover who had come all the way from the bottom of the earth, the land of big rocks and waves, to gather our grief into print, so he could purge his own. My beloved mid-life crisis Australian with the solemn green eyes, flecked with brown, and the perfect curve of brow. He who quoted Rilke and re-invented my Catholic angel by the light of the *gasera* at the foot of my mat. He gaped at my hair the first time I unbraided it for him. Hell, this is unreal, he murmured fervently, as if in a prayer, kissing the tips of my hair. "For beauty is nothing but the beginning of terror . . ."

He wept, was horrified and ashamed the first time he came to see me take my hair to the river on a wet high noon. The soldiers were restless while the whole village waited, each one praying, please, let it not be him, not my husband's body, or, *Santa Maria*, I'd rather it's my son this time, relieve this endless wait, time to come home now, or, *Madre de Dios*, let her be found at least still whole, ay, my most foolish youngest. And all hearts marking time at the bank, nearly breaking in unison as I, hair undone like a net, descended into the dark waters to fish out another victim of our senseless war.

*Desaparecidos*. Our disappeared, ay, so many of them. And the lovers left behind became obsessed with doors – one day, my son, daughter, husband or wife will be framed at the doorway. Behind the beloved will be so much light, and we shall be overcome by the fulfilment of our waiting.

They will come back – or will they? They did, one by one, through the water's door, from the darkness into the light.

And I served this homecoming. Fished out their bodies that returned from our river's whirlpool, deep down from the navel of the water, while the soldiers looked the other way. They could not understand why each body was so heavy, it always sank and never surfaced, until I rescued it. It seemed to want to vanish forever – no, each body only wants to become part of the water for a while, to make sure we never forget the taste of its being, Pay Inyo, the old grave-digger, said.

Perhaps he was right, for every time a new body was thrown furtively into the river, the water always changed flavour, no longer sweetened by the hills but tasting almost like brine, raw and sharp with minerals. Like fresh blood. Pay Inyo understood this to be the dead one's curse on memory, so that we would never forget him or her who had been loved.

You're crazy, your village is crazy, this is mad, a nightmare, why, how could you . . . this is not happening, I don't understand, I don't know . . . Tony wept on my wet, salty hair that had earlier wrapped the naked body of a sixteen-year-old *amazona*, a female guerilla. She hardly had any face left. Dark blotches, the size of a fist, covered her pelvis and breasts which had lost their nipples. In my hut, Tony raved, twisting my black rope around his arms and face as if wanting to shut out the vision. In his shock, he did not notice that my hair was growing several handspans longer; I was remembering for the dead the contours of her lost face. Tony was inconsolable.

I had to take him into my home, because Pay Inyo said he would not have a man gone mad in his house, it is bad luck, there's enough bad luck as it is. Besides, you're the one with some education, I only have crooked English, you know, the old man added. Ramon's eyes darkened when I led the sobbing Tony away from the bank where an eighty-year-old grandmother dumbly caressed the corpse's feet as if she were trying to remember something. I realised that, by then, my village had forgotten how to cry.

"Sissy Australian – *bakla*!" Ramon spat at Tony's back.

Back. My back, most loved. The night before he disappeared, Tony marvelled at how thin I was from behind. You people are so thin. Your vertebrae jut out, you know, he said, counting the ladders to my nape, kissing each bone, christening every hillock with the name of a gem. Sapphire, lapis lazuli, jade, ruby . . . often, I remembered his lips and the trail of precious stones on my back, and always my hair hurt.

But let's trade them for something more valuable than rungs of kisses, Tony, for something like fishes and loaves of bread – white or brown – like those in your country where it's easy to choose, because there are choices. The village has owned my hair, so why can't they have my bones as well?

"Time to go, Estrella, time to go . . ." Tony had hushed my bitter query.

After I fished out a boy's body, which nobody claimed, the cracks began to show. He must have been ten years old. The small head was thrown too far back, flopping behind him. Around his neck was a necklace of weeds and the fattest prawns. Thank god, it's not ours, but whose is it? We don't know. It must be from the next village. But it can't be one of the rebels, too tiny, too young. It is not "it!" I screamed, and for the first time the village that had forgotten how to cry, saw that perhaps I was beginning to remember how, behind all sockets, there can be no real drought for the eye.

You who read this and shiver at this macabre war, may you

never need to pretend that you have forgotten. And may you never know the kinship between fishing for the dead and actual killing. The first time you do either, you break. You, too, die within, thus you begin to practice the art of uncaring, teach your gut to behave for the sake of your own salvation, so that the next time and the next, it becomes easier to cross with mortality. Then you can at least breathe and thank heaven that it is not you who had fallen. But, somewhere at the tail-end of that numbed routine, you give once more. You break, and no amount of practice can put you back together again.

"I don't think I can do it again – ever," my voice was so hollow, one could knock at it and hear one's knuckles echoing through.

"*Putang ina*, you're getting soft, big hair." Ramon yanked at my braids. The black and red rope coiled at my feet.

"I might know who is – down there – I can't do it." Something was catching in my throat, I couldn't breathe.

"Why, you have e.s.p., too, woman?" Around his Adam's apple, the skin rippled as he laughed.

Before Tony arrived, I suspected that the sergeant had slyly desired me, maybe even worshipped me, in some grudging way, for my nerves of stone. After each dive, he would never look at what surfaced with me. He only stared at my brown body in the wet *tapis*, then at my face, always at my face, as if hoping to find some sign of breaking, for he never saw me weep over any of the corpses that I netted even when the whole riverbank howled. She has secret powers inside, Pay Inyo had said, thumping at his chest; in war, we need secret powers. No one knew that my hair stole all the grief from my face. How could anyone see the ache in my scalp, the trick of memory, the betrayal of nerves at the roots of my hair? Come to think of it, it's not my ancestry, not my father's Spanish blood, but the flush from the heart that had cursed the red into my hair.

My hair, the anchor for the remnants of a village, for the soldiers, and, later, for Tony. The disappeared could at least be found for a decent burial. And the river would be restored to its old taste, sweetened again by the hills. Then we could fish again or wash our clothes there again, or gather the *kangkong* and *gabi* leaves at its bank again. It meant sustenance, as food from the town had been scarce. Even the soldiers partly depended on the river for their daily needs. So why dump the bodies there? The soldiers said it wasn't them, they said the rain washed the bodies down to the river.

But how could you drink this, eat – my god! Tony gagged over the fish steamed in lemon grass after he witnessed the rescue of the young female guerilla. The following day, he refused to eat or drink. His limbs went cold and locked around him, then he developed a chill, even as his sweat soaked my mat. He became incoherent for weeks. Nearly deranged by his strange ailment, he would scream about the lemon grass fish growing fat and swimming inside the belly of the dead girl. I thought he was going to die. I wrapped him with my hair each night to keep him warm, then fell in love.

Another river swells on desperate nights like this, flowing in the pelvis. Strange how, when close to death, we become more intimate with desire. One tries to hide it, but this river overflows. Each night, when I hushed his cries and calmed his shaking, my *tapis* betrayed me, re-weaving its flowers into fishes that circled my hipbone which grew as luminous as the moon on the river, while the fishes swam to my breasts, biting behind the nipples. His cold, blue fingers reached for them, coaxing the fishes to leap out. Then, underneath my hair, he loved me over and over again, until the chill half-ebbed from his flesh, because I had shared it with mine – ay, dear reader, my scalp hurts again. I can hear the strands pushing out and stretching; it is the hum of memory, my beloved mumbling something about winter love in the tropics, his breath tinged with lemon grass.

"Was he that good?" Ramon grabbed me by the waist, and pulled me to him. His young breath travelled my face from brow to chin and back. "Really good?" he sniggered.

Yes, he was as good as any man who had come to the end of his journey, back to himself, but only to himself. I'll take you away, Tony had promised. I'll take you back with me, back to the light. And we will cut that hair.

Back to clean, sunny beaches where I could have long weekend breakfasts and gaze at the water that never changes flavour? Strange, lucky Aus-traayl-yuh, savoured in one lazy roll of the tongue – but not home, never home, Tony. He made ready to leave anyway, so he could arrange something for me, for us at his embassy. The sharpest pair of scissors to cut me off from my river.

As he was about to go, I unbraided my hair which he could not bear to see loose after he had recovered. I spread it around the house, hoping he would understand. You know Tony, all of this is destiny, I whispered as he left, but he never heard me. I saw lights in his eyes. He seemed happy, even inspired, perhaps at the thought of taking his lover home with her cropped mane. Time to go, he had said after we buried the ten-year-old's body together. He had rocked me to sleep then, wondering why there were no tears though my voice cracked with sorrow. Later, he noticed the faint streaks of white at my nape. "For beauty is nothing but the beginning of terror . . ." and we have no need of that, Estrella.

Lemon grass and fireflies this time, strange, but how beautiful, perhaps a miracle, perhaps salvation, one never knows, shards of the holy light of Damascus maybe, sent for the soldiers . . . and the river, *aysus*, it does not taste like fresh blood, not at all . . . Pay Inyo brought me the news. His bony frame, hunched at the bottom of my steps, was only a blur. But we want our river to taste only like our river, he made the point of his visit. I can't do it, no, please God, but I knew that I could not escape my final appointment. My hair awoke to the knowledge and my scalp ached as it had never ached before. I wanted to pull out every strand that heard my heart break then bang my head on the wall.

"He wasn't that good after all –" Ramon paused, slowing his words for effect. "Your pale sissy did not even know how to fight – like a man." He shoved his lips onto mine.

A stone sank in my womb. "You cur, you beast – *hayop ka!*" I bit his lips and kicked him in the groin, then lashed out with my braids of black and red, screaming, cur, cur, cur!

"*Putang ina!*" He tried to duck the blows as he cocked his rifle and yelled out to his men. The welts were blooming on his face and arms, the curse of my red lights.

"So you're the better man? Oh, yes, pull the trigger, brave Ramon," I sneered, gripping my whip of hair, eyes blurred and stinging.

"Ah, you cry after all, Fish-Hair Woman," the boy-sergeant smirked, deliberately laying down his weapon as he approached me. "But we'll need nerves for this job, won't we?" His voice was dangerously tender.

I raised my whip once more. His men cocked their rifles. I let my hair fall.

"In her heart, she knows she'll do it – don't you?" Ramon unbraided my hair slowly, taking great pleasure in smoothing it out into a net, for, as he suspected, that was the first time someone other than Tony and the dead had touched my hair. The men watched this defilement in absurd respect, and the fireflies returned, circling their guns, drawing halos.

We went, a grim procession to the river, guarded by a host of flying lights, the soldiers holding my hair like a bridal train. Again, I remembered his lips and the precious stones on my back and the river in my pelvis and his lemon grass fish swimming into it from the belly of a dead girl now growing her face and nipples back, and her grandmother rubbing her feet as if trying to remember something, and the soft mound of earth singing the ten-year-old bones to sleep.

Thus the betrayal of memory, while the soldiers mar-velled at how my hair grew and grew in their hands. They were in on the secret now. They knew that, once I dived into the waters sweet with lemon grass, I would never leave my heart on the bank again.

# COLOURS

Imagine a half-note about to drop from its stem. Imagine this departure from the possibility of song. This is how to fall out of love before it has even been declared. And then we leave, knowing we will never be called back.

She is all wept out now and I am depleted, but she will never know this. For a long time, my love for Maria was like an unfinished clef, a composition only about to begin, or merely a half-wish to begin. No, it was never put out there, not written as a score, and will never be played. I can't even say it was just a tune in my head. It was more of an inkling in my eyes, behind the sockets where I sensed a musical wish each time I saw her.

Her husband was a sallow man, very fine boned, ash-blond and reserved, an inward man. She was the opposite, dusky and robust, her manner always geared towards the superlative. She moved with an impetuous energy which echoed her choice of colours, sometimes a red bandanna on her hair, a garish yellow blouse or huge, blue earrings.

It must have been the red which made my eyes throb the first time I saw her. Maria was fashioning it like an exotic turban around her hair, but couldn't quite gather the stubborn tresses. The threat of a Southerly, and her on the roof – what was she doing there? Black hair and red bandanna struggled to fly from her head which was defiantly tilted back, lips parted as though she were drinking up the incoming storm. I stared for a long time, perhaps the first and last time I would see the precise contours of her face, and felt rather lost when she went back into the house.

At my fourth floor window I had to rest my eyes. A sharp contraction, no, a flush, a tingling. Eyes about to sing? My doctor looked at me strangely when I described the sensation. You're a very special case, he said. He dared not use the word "strange". Then he hypothesised about my condition. Bright colours might seem intense later on, only because of the growing blur around, but they might also hurt your eyes, so I suggest extra protection from any source of brightness, colours, harsh light, you know what I mean – and keep your window closed, he should have added.

Nowadays, I hardly open it. I stay away from that side of my flat which overlooks her roof and bedroom. I am all stared out, an ex-Peeping Tom, but without even a remnant of the eyes' sexual bravado to show for it. Just a handful of colours pushed far beyond the sockets. Perhaps, a red – or a yellow?

It was the only brightness that afternoon. I was at the busstop and the yellow ran towards me. All was grey, what with the rain and the shadows camped in my eyes – but the yellow kept running clearly towards me. I nearly held out a hand to ward off this assault of colour.

"I know you. You live next door – and you stare too much."

Nerves behind the eyes, literally. A tightening there. "That's a pretty yellow. Cheerful." I felt stupid saying that.

There was a touch of embarrassment in her laughter, or was it nervousness as I leaned closer?

"Yeah, cheerful and wet. Blasted rain." She stepped back, just as her face was coming into focus.

I stared at the yellow instead, attempting to obliterate the grey. "Cheerful and wet . . . ," I echoed, the familiar sensation as if italicised on my sockets.

She hugged the yellow with her arms, protectively. "Sad, old perv," she retorted and turned away. She thought I was ogling her breasts!

The bus saved me from the agony of composing an explanation. I didn't board it. I was more than embarrassed. I had offended her.

Orphaned at the bus-stop under a heavy downpour and feeling diminished, and explaining to myself, eyes about to sing, eyes about to sing. My sockets were curved like notes that didn't quite come full circle, and on their inadequate curvature, an urgent palpitation insinuated itself.

My doctor said I needed dark glasses for protection. I ignored his advice. I didn't want the world to grow any darker. I wanted only to dream of yellow breasts. Perhaps, she was right about me being a sleazebag, but I couldn't help it. The shapes, which I could no longer see clearly, became more defined in an inkling of song the hue of mangoes, daffodils, jonquils, all yellow staring back at me. The strange man from the fourth floor window honoured by a look, but never by any invitation to sing, because she had a husband and I was only a pair of disreputable eyes next door.

Consider the gaze under suspicion. Is it intrinsically perverted, or does it become perverse in the eyes of the beholder? After that yellow encounter, I began watching her bedroom window, and I was ashamed of myself, especially because the nights became unbearable. Behind my eyes, then bearing down on my chest and soon locked in my pelvis was an exquisite ripeness. I began to sleep naked.

The roof, the bus-stop, then finally my doorstep. How do I map out the progress of the gaze and everything unsaid about it, that which I cannot yet hold in contempt, because it's still incomprehensible? Roof, bus-stop, doorstep coming to a head. Only three major occasions, but how my sightings of Maria developed and what eventually happened behind my sockets on the third encounter were undeniable. Unnotated, of course, not yet articulate like full knowledge, but true – I had fallen in love.

Such primary landmarks. Awe, desire, love. Red, yellow, blue.

Because she was so close, I saw that this blue was both dark and bright. Big, shiny plates of it. A blue armour on each ear, perhaps to guard it from hearing my urge to sing. That time, it was not a mere tremor, but an ache which a more able man could have transposed into the saddest concerto.

It was Christmas eve. She knocked on my door at about one a.m., wearing her unnaturally large, blue earrings, just as I was drifting off to another yellow sleep. She was crying. My husband, no one to help, the guests have left, come quickly, please, she begged.

Perhaps, blue is the colour of love.

In the ambulance, all the way to the hospital, when her tears were shifting into focus and blurring then shifting into focus again, I concentrated on the blue instead, hoping it would save me from that wretched yearning. She held his hand. I longed to hold hers, to hold her.

Blue is both bright and dark, the sky and the ocean; at the

bottom, it's almost black. Notate that vision for me, please, I could have asked her that, but I never had the chance nor the courage to sing. I could only stare.

A week later, she wore black. She hid the red, yellow and blue, rolled up the signposts in my little story, which she didn't even know existed.

At the funeral, she laid a hand on my arm and murmured her thanks. I was sporting dark glasses and a cane for the first time. She asked whether I had hurt myself or something, then went off to receive more condolences.

I knew she wore an unrelieved black that day, but it no longer mattered. Behind my eyes, the light had been nearly switched off. Any bright colour would have been lost on me.

For a month or so, I tried to make contact, to catch her eye, what an absurd wish. But maybe she never went up the roof again, or she might have kept her bedroom blinds drawn forever, then gotten herself a car and never took the bus again. She could have even uprooted her house from the staring man's vision, who knows, but it wouldn't have mattered.

Nowadays, my window remains closed. Three years after the vision on the roof, the light is completely out, or so I thought, until the blur of her face sneaked into my room again, so I decided to tell this story, I hope you don't mind. Yes, just last night, Maria up close, weeping in the ambulance. Tear on her lash – a half-note about to drop from its stem? Vaguely, I remember dismissing it as a limp metaphor before I drifted off to a sound, prosaic sleep.

# STORM

I'm afraid, during the storm last night, a falling coconut frond pierced my heart and let the north-wind in. It was so sudden. He had just begun snoring beside me, him limp and wet on my hip as he gripped my thighs with his long, hairy leg, when part of the roof and a coconut frond crashed on my bed. I thought I was unhurt, though shaking in terror by then. He kept on sleeping. He only shifted, changed his snore rhythm and gripped my thighs tighter.

He had been drinking hard, downing his usual *tuba* at the end of the table, while I cleared the supper which he did not touch. *Amo* said he had some *lomi* at Gloria's house, so he wasn't hungry. He had arrived soaking wet from the storm and in a mood more foul than the last time. The past nights after his engagement to Gloria, he came home looking grim and cursing under his breath heavy with *tuba*. He always returned with a bottle which he finished through supper. And during the meal, always the old question.

"Hoy, Viring, don't I treat you well, pay you well?" His gruff voice punctuated the howling of the northwind among the coconut trees. I wondered about my mother and brothers back in Iraya. Must be flooded there again –

"Hoy, didn't you hear me? I want you to tell me whether I treat you well?"

*Amo* was a generous master. When he first hired me to keep house for him, because he wanted Gloria to think he was rich enough to afford a maid, he gave my mother a thousand pesos as an advance for my first two months. On my fourteenth birthday, I made my first thousand – ay, was I proud! I kissed my mother and little brothers goodbye and promised to be good.

"Hoy, I'm talking to you!"

"*Opo, Amo*, you're a good master."

"And I always pay you on time, don't I? DON'T I?" He had to raise his voice above a sudden gale which hissed through the slightly open window.

"On time, *Amo*."

"Will you shut that window properly . . . the latch, DON'T FORGET THE LATCH . . . that's better – I can hardly hear myself in my own house. *Lintian*, this storm is proving to be the devil himself!"

Ay, our poor village. I had felt the northwind on my breast while I closed that window. It seemed to pound its way through my heart. *Amo* is right, the storm is a bad one. After this, I'll have to ask him for some advance pay again. Our hut will need a new roof and new wall, yes, the northern wall, of course –

"And how much is your salary?"

When the coconut trees keen like old women tearing at their hair, I can't help but think of home . . .

"*Ano ka, bungog*? Hoy, Viring, I'm talking to you – you, deaf?"

"I'm sorry, *Amo* – what was it that you said?" I hurriedly began to clear the rice from the table. Have to finish soon. With this storm and *Amo* in this mood, I'd rather be in bed.

"I asked how much I pay you," his voice tailed me to the kitchen.

"Five hundred a month, *Amo*."

"Come back here, will you? We're having a proper conversation, girl. Hoy, come back, I said – CAN'T YOU HEAR ME?"

I rushed back in, but stood at the other end of the table, waiting for his next questions which I knew so well – the wind tormented the latch.

"Pay attention when I'm talking to you, ha? And you're happy with that – that pay, I mean? And you promise to stay on and serve your mistress well after we get married?"

"Yes, *Amo*."

"Yes what?"

"Yes, I'm happy and I promise to stay . . ."

"Now tell that to Gloria! *Lintian*, she's probably having second thoughts about the wedding, because I told her she can't bring her personal maid to my household! I have you, what more can she ask? Ay, that darkie of hers gets under my skin, she and her devotion to her mistress."

The window shuddered from a blast of rain.

"*Buli ni'na niya*! This storm is driving me nuts! I bet you, Darkie's hovering around her mistress again, probably in her bedroom – *lintian*, you never know what happens in a storm like this! Ah, she's probably propping up her pillows or combing her hair – she combs her hair, can you believe – ?"

The window seemed to sag inwards with the weight of the wind.

"You made sure of the latch, ha?"

"Yes, *Amo*."

"And do you think it's right for a maid to be too close to her mistress?"

"No, *Amo*."

He used to rant about Gloria's personal maid all the time. She never leaves her mistress, he'd say, and she's always touching her, arranging her dress, doing her hair, or wiping her back, even in front of him. And her dark hand would linger on her mistress' skin every time! I always got embarrassed when he talked this way.

"Like today. She would not leave us alone when we were having *merienda*. She pretended she was shooing the flies away or serving Gloria's snack – *buli ni'na niya*, she was giving me the evil eye all the time, I know. I could not even touch my own *nobya*, or kiss her . . . I tried, but, imagine, Darkie screamed! She screamed – isn't that mad, Viring? ISN'T THAT MAD?"

I attempted to escape to the kitchen with the plate of gingered fish, but he caught my arm. The latch rattled again and again, and the coconut trees keened even louder. I stared at the untouched fish and wondered what Mamay and the kids were having for supper.

"I'm asking you a question, girl!"

"Yes, *Amo*?"

"You're a good maid, Viring, but you know what your problem is? You're deaf. DEAF!"

"Sorry, *Amo*, sorry *po*." I tried to head back to the kitchen, but his hand tightened around my arm. Outside, a coconut tree crashed to the ground.

"But at least you're rather pretty and fair. Yes, you'll look good beside your mistress – she's so *mestiza*, you know, and seeing that darkie's hand on her makes my blood boil!"

When *Amo* went to our village to look for a maid, he specified that he wanted a nice, fair-skinned, young girl, because he liked seeing a fresh and clean thing around the house. My mother smiled and proudly presented me to him. Ay, Mamay! She and the kids must be wading on knee-high water by now. *Dios mio*, how can they sleep then . . . ?

"Yes, I like seeing a fresh and clean thing around the house. Sit, girl, sit." He giggled and forced me to sit beside him. I nearly fell as he tugged me down. The gingered fish landed on my lap and the plate broke on the floor.

Then the lights went out.

"*LINTIAN*, BROWN-OUT AGAIN! *LINTIAN*!"

"*Amo, Amo*, if you . . . if you let me go, I can get some candles . . ."

"NO! Stay here, stay beside me. I like you close this way, in the dark," he giggled again, making popping noises in his throat.

"*Amo* . . . the candles . . . I can get some, you know . . ."

"Did I tell you she's as dark as a – as a brown-out?" He giggled even more and moved closer.

"Fish, fish, I caught a fish alive!" His other hand groped for the fish on my lap and stayed there. "Why is my Viring trembling so? You don't like fish?"

"*Amo*, please, . . . let me clean up this mess . . . and some light . . . I must . . . please let me go . . ."

"Ah, I don't need candles to know you're nearly as white as my Gloria . . . even then, I don't like your hand on your mistress, ha? You will serve me, then your mistress. I pay your five hundred, not your mistress, understand?"

"Yes, *Amo*, but, *Amo*, I have to clean up . . . please . . ."

"Viring," he breathed hotly on my cheek. "I couldn't even kiss my wife-to-be, because her maid screamed. Isn't that crazy? But you don't scream, do you? Do you?"

"*Amo*, please, please, no, . . ."

The latch rattled like a demented throat.

"You don't like fish, so I'll clean you up . . ." He locked an arm around my neck and removed the fish from my thigh. "Look what you've done. All the nice sauce on your thighs . . . sweet ginger, isn't it . . . ?" He snickered, rubbing the sauce on my lips.

Again and again, the wind blasted the window.

"No, *Amo*, please, *Amo* . . . *ay, Madre de Dios!*"

"I like thighs, you know, fresh and clean thighs . . . I've been wanting to do this . . . this and this . . . feel my Gloria's white, white thighs, . . . but nothing escaped Darkie . . . nothing escaped that *buli ni'na niya* . . . that, that cunt of her mother!"

Nothing escaped me either, as I hunted for the coconut frond that pierced my heart and let the northwind in – my bruised breasts, the blood between my thighs, on his limp thing and all over my blanket . . . and more coconut fronds than I could ever imagine, peering down through that hole on the roof. Ay, how could anything escape me after it was over, when I saw it all a few hours ago? Even when I shut my eyes the whole time he grunted like a pig on top of me, I saw his face clearly, even his eyes. And I saw them in there, heard them even, rows and rows of coconut trees keening. His twenty hectares of old women, all tearing their hair in the wind.

Ay, Mamay of God, they screamed at me to get up, but I couldn't! He was so heavy – and as strong as a crazed *diablo*. He kept on calling out Gloria's name and cursing her maid at the same time, while he dug into me. I must have fainted, because I thought I felt the coconut trees lashing at me with their hair, howling with the wind, "Wake up, wake up!"

When I woke to the crashing roof, I knew my heart was wounded. And a coconut frond, an old woman's strand of green hair, had done it! You have to believe me, because I saw the frond coated with my own blood and felt my chest nearly bursting, my heart billowing with the northwind. I knew, because the storm suddenly stopped outside. Because my heart had sucked it all in through its red mouth, a tiny hole the width of a coconut frond.

I found it and knew I would never be the same again. Ay, listen to me, especially not after a heartstorm drove me outside the house to gather more coconut fronds, the sharpest of green hair. Not after his twenty hectares of old women began keening in my breast, "Dig into his skin! Drive each frond into him!"

Into his brow, on each of his eyes, through his jugular, heart, elbows, palms, belly, groin, thighs, down to his feet – *Madre de Dios*! I wondered why there was so little blood, if at all, except of course on the groin. And that was not even his.

# WHITE TURTLE

I'll dream you a turtle tonight;
cradle on her back
bone-white.
I'll dream you a turtle tonight.

Lola Basyon listened intently to the translation of the final
lines from her chanted story, then to the palms which met
in loud approval in the foyer of an art deco building in
Sydney. She was very pleased. Her translator, an Australian
anthropologist, was doing an excellent job. They must like
the story or turtles or dreams, or the sound of dreams in
their own tongue, the seventy-year-old chanter from the
Philippines thought, as she bowed politely to the crowd,
hand on her heart.

Filipina storyteller and chanter Salvacion Ibarra, a.k.a.
Lola Basyon, was on her road to fame, but she didn't know
this, nor did she care. Her main concern was to get the
night over with.

"Please – can't you sing those last lines again in your

dialect – Bikol, isn't it? It's beautiful . . ." said the woman at the other end of the stage.

Ay, the oriole with the books that made people laugh. Lola Basyon turned towards the bright yellow streak on the black hair which was neatly combed back from a half-awed face. Of the three authors who read from their books that night, the old woman liked best this vivacious young writer with her silver bangles and vivid gear. She reminded her of a rare bird in the forest back home. A glossy oriole.

But the novelist who sported a cowboy hat and snakeskin boots disturbed the old chanter. She kept an eye on his boots under the table, worrying that anytime they might slither all over the stage. He had a way of running his fingers over the crisp pages of his book, almost lovingly, before he began reading. He hardly looked at anyone or anything except the fine print of his text. He stared at it so hard that Lola Basyon wondered whether he had a problem with his eyes, poor man. The other author, a middle-aged man with grey sideburns and dark, heavy spectacles, was very polite, she observed, as he, half-smiling, nodded to whoever had finished reading. He himself had read for more than half an hour and, being last, Lola Basyon wondered whether they would ever get to her turn. She was very nervous; she felt she didn't quite belong. With no book or even paper to cling to, she hid her hands under the folds of her *tapis*. She imagined the audience could hear them shake; she had been worried since the program began. How in the world would they see the white turtle if I can conjure it only in my dialect? Ay, *Dios ko*, this is very difficult indeed.

The old woman rubbed the fabric of her *tapis* between her fingers for luck. She had chosen to wear her dead mother's *fiesta* clothes, because they had always made her feel as if she were wrapped in a cosy blanket but, at the same time, dressed for a special occasion. The *tapis* was home-dyed in various shades of soft green. The blouse, a *kimona* made of *piña*, the fibres of pineapple leaves, was embroidered with tiny *sampaguita* blooms and intricate loops at the neck and sleeves. But this finery seemed to lose its old power of bestowing comfort and confidence when the storyteller stepped into the big building of strange, white faces. For a while, she did not know what to do with her shaking hands.

Oriole's reassuring smile from the other end of the table had eased her anxiety, and now the black hair with its vibrant yellow plumage was nodding towards her. "Please – I'd love to hear it again. It's very beautiful."

"*Salamat* . . . thank you . . ." Lola Basyon bowed once more. She understood "beautiful", but couldn't quite comprehend the request in the foreign tongue. She turned to the anthropologist who immediately came to her aid. The chanter obliged.

> *Ngunyan na banggi*
> *ipangaturugan taka ki pawikan;*
> *duyan sa saiyang likod*
> *kasingputi kang buto.*
> *Ngunyan na banggi*
> *ipangaturugan taka ki pawikan.*

All palms, especially Oriole's, responded with enthusiasm once again. Except Cowboy's. He was still glued to his book, scanning it for the next round of readings. There was a faint buzz of praise in the room. Lola Basyon felt the warmth rippling in her stomach then invading her arms, flushing her hands to their fingertips. She abandoned her *tapis* and lay her hands on the table.

"*Salamat . . . maraming salamat . . .* thank you very much." They saw the white turtle after all, thank God. They're talking about it now.

"Imagine, doing harmonies in her throat."

"It's like listening to three voices singing. Amazing."

"I've never heard anything quite like that before. An unusual way to produce sound, don't you think so?"

Lola Basyon was tired though exhilarated. She had just flown in from the Philippines the day before for this writers' festival. The Australian anthropologist, after so much fussy discussions with the board, had arranged that she be invited to this event. He had met her during his research on the mythologised genesis of native peoples, and was undoubtedly charmed.

In her village of Iraya, he had fallen in love with her chant about the white turtle. Its story is pure poetry, he had explained to her in broken Bikol, his blue eyes misting over, growing as bright as the sea where the turtle swam. A mythical tale – once the turtle was small and blue-black, shiny like polished stones. It was an unusual creature even then; it had a most important task. It bore on its back the dreams of Iraya's dead children as it dived to the navel of the sea. Here, it buried little girl and boy dreams that later sprouted into corals which were the colour of bones. After many funerals, it began to grow bigger and lighter in colour; eventually it, too, became white, bone-white. This was Lola Basyon's story, told in a chant. When the anthropologist first heard it, he felt as if the white turtle had somersaulted into his eyes.

That night of the readings, it dived into him again, down to the depth of his irises, as he acted as interpreter. After she sang each scene, he would read his translation. Theirs was a dialogue in two tongues blending and counterpointing. Strange to hear the turtle voice in English, Lola Basyon thought. She rather liked its sound though –

> I am your cradle
> rocking

> your babydreams
> past anemone;
> the hundred fingers
> curling
> around sleepgurgles
> passing . . .

What an exciting version of performance poetry! A group from the back row tuned their ears more to the chanting than to the translated story. Notice how she sings with no effort at all. She doesn't even blink her eyes.

> *Ako ang simong duyan*
> *napasagid*
> *sa puting kurales . . .*
>
> I am your cradle
> brushing
> against white corals;
> porous bones
> draw in
> your bubblebreath
> humming.

Oriole's eyes were closed. She was engulfed by the chant, lulled into it, falling into the sea with the anthropologist and some keen listeners to his English translation. Wonder how this feels in her dialect for someone who is born to it –

> I sail your cradle home.
> Be water.
>
> I sink your cradle
> deep beyond grief.
> Be stone.

The bespectacled writer was slightly impatient – but her act is a multicultural or indigenous arts event, definitely not for a writers' festival. And those organisers should have, at least, printed and handed out the translation to the audience. That anthropologist's reading is painfully wooden, dead. And this could go on forever, heaven forbid. He looked at his watch, shaking his head –

> But warm. Skin-smooth
> and promising wings.
> Be bird.
>
> And hear your flapping
> from the navel of the sea.

Cowboy was bored. He was suspicious of all performance poetry. He thought it was invented to disguise pedestrian writing. Where he came from, he had seen too many performance poets outshouting, outstyling each other. He fixed his gaze at the cover of his latest crime fiction.

"Nice performance – and what a fabulous top." A woman in black and pearls whispered to her companion in the front row as the anthropologist ended the reading of his translation. She could not take her eyes off Lola Basyon's *piña* blouse.

"Wonder what it's made of."

"Very fine material, I'd say."

"I love your story. It's poetry – where can we get your book?" A teenage boy wearing a pony-tail addressed the chanter directly in order to drown the clothes-talk at his elbow. He's about the age of my favourite grandson back home, Lola Basyon thought. She couldn't help but notice him. Earlier, right after her chant, he had placed two fingers into his mouth and whistled, then he had clapped vigorously, stamping his feet. She felt embarrassed, but pleased. Did you see the white turtle, she wanted to ask him.

"I'd like a copy of your book. It would be a treasure."

A faint titter issued from the back row.

Book, book. Lola Basyon understood the word, but what was he after – "Book . . . ?"

Cowboy rolled his eyes to heaven then back to his latest

crime fiction and the bespectacled author raised his brows towards a tall woman in cobalt blue. She was the chair of the readings.

"Yes, book – your book. I'd like very much to buy –"

The anthropologist tried to intervene, but Lola Basyon was just beginning to speak, so he kept quiet.

"Book . . ."

"Yes, book . . ."

"*Gusto niya raw bumili ng libro mo*," a shrill voice from the audience interrupted the exchange. "Excuse me, I'm a journalist from the Philippine community paper here in Sydney – and I was just translating for her that young man's request," she addressed everyone before taking a photo of Lola Basyon and sitting down. The anthropologist-translator felt censured.

"I'd love a copy, yes . . ." the young man pressed on.

The storyteller sensed the blue sleeve at her shoulder. The chair of the readings was explaining that the audience would have enough time to chat with the writers during drinks later and that they were running out of time, but she was interrupted by the young man's seatmate.

"Do you have a publisher here?"

Cowboy suppressed a giggle, the spectacles adjusted and re-adjusted themselves – she shouldn't have been in this panel in the first place – and Oriole looked very disconcerted.

"I like your white turtle very much."

Now who is it this time? All heads turned towards the origin of the very young voice. A girl, about six, stood on her chair at the back of the foyer and made her own statement, "Oh, yes, I do."

Her mother shushed her, but she was very determined –

"Is it really white . . . ?"

In broken Bikol, the anthropologist tried to explain to the

storyteller just what was happening, while the cobalt blue dress took the floor and, with admirable diplomacy, introduced the second half of the readings. The embarrassed mother had to drag her protesting daughter out of the building. "But I've got lots of questions," she bawled.

Cowboy caressed his pages again and cleared his throat before launching into his old spiel, with improvisations this time. He rhapsodised over more details on the writing of his latest novel. How he was converted to crime fiction, but not the genre writing kind, mind you. He was a committed anti-gun lobbyist. His heroes were good cowboys like him, someone like the Lone Ranger without a gun. Oriole and the older writer seemed very amused, while from the audience the Filipina journalist took another photo of Lola Basyon staring at the speaker's snakeskin boots.

After the reading, a lively exchange of impressions filled the foyer. The exquisite poetic style of the older writer, the quirky plots in Cowboy's fiction and Oriole's comic eroticism were notable conversation pieces. And, of course, Lola Basyon's extraordinary chanting was also a favoured subject. Almost like three voices harmonising in her throat, remember? A few referred to the awkward moment when the boy asked about the old woman's publication. How silly, how ridiculously dumb, the woman in pearls complained to the anthropologist. He had put that poor thing in an embarrassing situation.

The drinks taste very strange, but these colourful bits are so delicious – *siram sana*! Oblivious to all the murmurings about her, "the poor thing" was having the time of her life sampling all, from the wine to the orange juice to the trays of canapés and fruit as the crowd made a beeline for the three authors' book-signing.

I wish I had understood their stories, she thought, shaking her head while biting into a strawberry. They must be very important ones considering how fat their books are. Ay, impressive indeed. She ran her fingers across the books, imitating Cowboy's loving gesture, then parked herself beside the food trays.

"*Marhay ta* enjoy *ka. Su kanta mo* very good." The anthropologist offered her another glass of orange juice. He said he was glad to see her having a good time and that the audience loved her story.

"*Kumusta*, I'm Betty Manahan, a Filipina journalist originally from Manila. *Ang galing mo talaga* – great performance!" She hugged and kissed the chanter then shook the anthropologist's hand before adjusting her camera. "I'll put you on the front page of my paper," she gushed at Lola Basyon. "I can make you famous in Sydney, you know – isn't she fantastic?"

"She's very special," the anthropologist agreed. "Her turtle story is just – just beyond me. I must say I –"

"I liked your translation, too – could you take our photo, please?" The journalist handed the camera to the enthusiastic translator before posing beside Lola Basyon, who looked a bit baffled.

"Picture *tayo*." The journalist flashed her most engaging smile at the old woman and towards the camera, putting an arm around the waist of her greatest discovery.

A quarter of an hour later, after many more compliments, Lola Basyon found herself alone beside the food trays. I must memorise the taste of this wonderful feast, so I could tell it to my grandchildren. Imagine, they put pink fish on biscuits and what's this yellow thing that smells like old milk, I don't like it, ay, ay. And what's that blowing bubbles over there? Someone had just popped a champagne bottle open. *Aprubicharan ngani*, I'll try it, too. *Hoy, luway-*

*luway daw*, Basyon, easy, easy, she chided herself, or else they might think you're very *ignorante*.

"Thanks for that fabulous performance."

In the middle of gulping the bubbly thing, Lola Basyon recognised the pearled woman who had kept staring at her *kimona* blouse earlier. The chanter smiled up at her. *Aysus*, how very tall.

"That's beautiful, very delicate . . ." The woman gestured towards the *kimona*.

"Beautiful." Lola Basyon bowed and pointed to the other's pearls.

The woman smiled graciously. "What's it made of?" she asked, squinting at the *kimona*.

"*Sige, kaputi ngani* . . . touch . . . touch . . ." The chanter held out the edge of her blouse towards the manicured fingers.

The pearls leant forward and fondled the floral embroidery. "I say, so dainty, so . . ."

"Mother . . . my mother . . ." With little success, the storyteller was trying to tell her about the source of the heirloom when the pony-tailed young man appeared. He had just extricated himself from the long book-signing queue.

"Thank you very, very much for your story . . ." he began.

The pearls excused herself. "I guess I must join the queue now," she told him and laid a hand on the chanter's arm. "See you."

"I do like your song immensely." The young man's face was unabashedly radiant.

Somehow, Lola Basyon understood this overflow of enthusiasm and youthful confidence – the way he opens his hands towards me like my favourite grandson. She managed the widest grin; her jaws ached pleasantly. He smiled back.

"I wish I could tell you how I feel about the burial of

dreams of dead children. How I really feel about your story – here," he said, cupping his hand to his chest.

"Story . . . sad . . . happy." She scanned her head for more English words.

"Sad-happy, you're quite right, and very disturbing."

She longed so much to understand the full meaning of his earnestness. And she wanted to ask whether he saw the white turtle, but how to say it. She looked around for the anthropologist so he could translate for her, but he was chatting with the chair of the readings. And the Filipina journalist was busy "networking with my Aussie VIPs, you know."

Again, the young man opened his arms towards her. "I like the sound of your dialect, too. I wish I could have a copy of your story, but –"

Ay, my son, why don't you speak my tongue? Lola Basyon longed for a proper conversation with this beaming face. "Story . . . ?"

"I know, I know, stupid of me. Of course, that was an oral story . . . how could I have made a fool of myself then? And look at me now trying to . . ."

"Excuse me, please . . ."

Lola Basyon felt a slight tug at her skirt from behind.

"Is it really white, your turtle?"

She turned to face the bold little girl who had asked about the turtle earlier. Her eyes were shining.

"Really white white?"

"White turtle . . ." This Lola Basyon understood.

"There you are. I thought I'd find you here." The mother took her daughter's hand. "Thanks very much for your performance. We loved it."

"Big turtle?" The girl drew a large circle with her little hands.

Lola Basyon chuckled, nodding vigorously, "Big . . . big big."

"White white, too."

"White white," the chanter repeated, squatting before the child.

"And beautiful?"

"Beautiful." She opened her arms towards the girl as if to embrace her, but she clung to her mother.

"You're all shy now, hey?" The mother laughed.

"Beautiful," Lola Basyon laughed, too, pointing at the daughter.

For the first time since she boarded the plane from her country, the old chanter felt very relaxed. She was making a real conversation at last. She will tell her grandchildren just how nice these people are. And they saw the turtle, after all, they really saw it. *Ay, I could sing for them forever.*

With her second glass of champagne and amidst this comforting company, the old woman was transported back home, close to the forest and the sea of her village, among her grandchildren begging for the old story, waiting for her to take them for a swim on the turtle's back. All in a night's chant.

> *Ngunyan na banggi*
> *ipangaturugan taka ki pawikan;*
> *duyan sa saiyang likod*
> *kasingputi kang buto.*
> *Ngunyan na banggi*
> *ipangaturugan taka ki pawikan.*

The warmth in her stomach made double-ripples as she began to chant again, filling her lungs with the wind from the sea and her throat with the sleepgurgles of anemones. Her cheeks tingled sharply with saltwater. "I'll dream you a turtle tonight –" she sang softly at first, then steadily raised her volume, drowning the chatter in the foyer.

Three harmonising voices reverberated in the room with

more passion this time, very strange, almost eerie, creating ripples in everyone's drink. All book-signing stopped. People began to gather around the chanter. By the time the main door was pushed open from outside by a wave of salty air, the whole foyer was hushed. An unmistakable tang pervaded it – seaweed!

"White white . . . oh, look . . . beautiful white!"

The little girl saw it first, its bone-white head with the deep green eyes that seemed to mirror the heart of the sea and the wisdom of many centuries. It was as large as the four-seater table from where the three authors stared in bewildered silence. Taking in the crowd, the white turtle raised its head as if testing the air. Then it blinked and began to make turtle sounds, also in three voices harmonising in its throat and blending with the song of the chanter. Everyone craned their necks towards the newly arrived guest.

Six voices now sending ripples through everyone's drink. *Hesusmaryahosep*, the Filipina journalist muttered under her breath, a miracle! The mother and daughter, and the young man gasped as the immense creature came very close, while, at the other end of the room, the anthropologist stood riveted, all movement drawn in, pushed to the back of his eyes. A hundred white turtles somersaulted there.

Whatta gimmick, a regular scene-stealer, Cowboy thought as he left the book-signing table and strode towards the very late guest, peeved but as curious as everyone. Meanwhile, the older writer, sideburns strangely tightening against his cheeks, peered from his spectacles and Oriole sensed the salt-sting behind her eyes. "Ohs" and "ahs" travelled the foyer while the hand of the woman, who loved the *kimona*, flew to the pearls in her throat and the cobalt blue dress hugged itself, swaying to the chant.

The skin around everyone's ears tingled.

As if in choreographed motion, all bodies began to lean towards the two chanters, arms stretched out, palms open, raring to catch each of the six voices. Even Cowboy had succumbed to this pose which was almost like a prelude to a petrified dive or dance. For a brief moment, everyone was still.

"Can I pat it?"

The girl had wriggled free from her mother. "Can I?" Her voice, in its foreign tongue and timbre, wove into the long, drawn-out vowels of the chant.

But the mother heard her daughter distinctly above the alien ululations. She grabbed the eager hand and held her close, hugging her tightly. The dreams of dead children, the mother remembered, goosebumps growing on her arm. Why am I being so silly?

"I want to pat it. I want to touch – it's a good turtle, a beautiful, good turtle," the child protested, beginning to cry.

The spell was broken. Everyone started moving and speaking in unison, some in wonder, others with the deepest unnameable emotions, but a few murmured their doubts. Dreams? Dead children? Suddenly, they remembered the story. Funerals. One man contemptuously dismissed this foolishness and argued instead against cruelty to animals. It was probably flown all the way here. Part of the act? Just look at that poor, strange, beautiful thing, an endangered species, no doubt. But what if it had been smuggled in? speculated an elderly woman. It might not have even been quarantined – the crowd began dispersing. In the din, the turtle stopped singing and Lola Basyon swallowed her voice.

Silent now, the massive whiteness crawled towards the table where the books were displayed. Passing the snakeskin boots of Cowboy, it seemed to shudder and hesitate before moving on. The chair of the readings rushed out of the room to ring for help.

When the police arrived, they found it nestling its head on the old woman's lap beside the table of books. They were dumbstruck. What whiteness, what extraordinary, beautiful whiteness. Colour of bone. And with eyes full of understanding as they stared at the last two people in the room. By then, everyone had been asked to clear the area. Only Lola Basyon and the anthropologist were left behind.

She wanted to explain to the men in blue that it did not mean to cause harm or any trouble, that perhaps it came to the reading because she did not have a book. Because the story that she chanted was written only on its back, never really hers. Only lent to her in a moment of music. She wanted to plead for them to be gentle with it. It was very tired after a long, long swim. But how to be understood, how to be heard in one's own tongue.

It blinked its emerald eyes at the police. It seemed sad, as if it were in mourning. Its white back stirred, then rocked like an inverted cradle. The anthropologist sensed the burial of dreams. Gloved hands steadying the creature, the police wondered about the unnameable emotion that stirred in their wrists, a strange, warm ripple of sorts. They lifted it with utmost tenderness as if it were a holy, precious thing. It was as large as the table, but oh so light.

# MACDO

I am twenty-seven and this is my first time. It's also my sister's first time. She's eighteen.

"Good morning, ma'am. How are you today? May I help you?" chirps the young girl at the counter, in very well-enunciated English.

"Uh-huh, what would you like, Rosa?" I nudge my sister.

"Whatever you like –" She's overtaken by severe coughing.

"Okay *ka*?" I rub her back. I sense a hollow kick with each cough.

"Just barking again, don't worry." Rosa is hunched over her palms, trying to muffle the sound.

The young girl steps back slightly, still smiling, and politely pursues our transaction. "So what would you like, ma'am?"

"Uhmm . . . maybe, uhmmm, I don't know." I hear synchronised fidgeting from the long queue behind me. "What do you have?"

She never loses her chirpiness as she enumerates the lot in singsong: "Big Mac, Quarter-pounder, fries, apple pie . . ." etc., etc.

"Do you have a – a small Mac?" I fondle the two tightly folded hundred-peso bills in my pocket.

"Small Mac?" The girl smiles overbrightly. "Not really, ma'am."

There is a slight titter in the queue.

"We just want the simplest hamburger, please, no *borloloy* –" No frills, more like a sensible meal, yes, that's what I mean.

An impatient tut-tut behind us.

"Well, ma'am, I think you'll enjoy our regular hamburger then –"

"How much?"

"Fifteen pesos . . . actually, all the prices are up there." Lisa indicates the large billboard. Her name-badge shines under the bright fluorescent.

"One regular hamburger then and a Coke, no, make it two regulars and one Coke, no, make it two Cokes, I think?"

"Yes, two regulars and two Cokes." Rosa has recovered. She even finished the mental computation which I was trying to make in relation to our other expenses for the afternoon.

"So, two regular hamburgers and two Cokes," Lisa reiterates our order, as though we would deny it.

A sigh of relief from the queue.

Ms MacLisa hands me the change and beams in her very neat uniform. "Enjoy your meal, ma'am."

I can't handle charm, so I simply shuffle out of the queue, my sister in tow.

"Spoken-ing English – ma'am?" Out of earshot, I mock the language and demeanour of our sweet server. I'm not being fair; of course, she's working with the nicest golden arches.

"Spoken-ing dollar, ma'am." A joke between Rosa and I – to speak English is to speak dollar. "Very high-class *siyempre*, ma'am." Nose upturned, Rosa flicks her hands fastidiously before swooping at the grub.

We both have a good laugh, while munching our very first McDonald's hamburgers.

Rosa is unusually thin. There are shadows under her eyes, giving her a wide-eyed look, as if she were anticipating the world to surprise her. I have a very pretty sister.

"This is okay."

"This is different."

To say the least. We hardly eat out and, when we do, only if it's my payday, we choose the smallest noodle stand parked among the hawkers in the market. Usual fare: only one bowl of noodles, and may we have an extra bowl and spoon, please, then one pork-bun plus a Coke to wash down the meticulously halved meal. *Hating-kapatid* – halved-for-sisters, meaning everything equally divided, the same soup-level in the two bowls and a couple of perfect half-moons out of the bun. Sometimes, I let Rosa cheat a little. She used to be hungry all the time.

"Hoy, eat, eat up," I say, seeing that she's left half of her burger untouched. "C'mon, Rosa, no leftovers now." We can't shame our first MacDo – pronounced with a glottal stop in the "o", as if your throat suddenly got clogged with fries, yes, something like that. MacDo. Local nickname for McDonald's.

"I was hungry, but I'm not now –" she's coughing again and knocking at her breast with a fist, as if chastising her own body.

"*Mea culpa, mea culpa*," I say, her mannerism irritating me.

She laughs and covers her mouth with one hand, while waving the food and me away from her with the other.

Loss of appetite, weight, sleep, plus night-fevers and coughing, severe coughing, especially at night. We've been careful though. We make it a point to sleep in opposite positions, her feet beside my head and vice versa, that sort of "safe" arrangement on the small bed in our rented room with the grilled window that looks out to a high wall, one can hardly see the sky. Sometimes, if we're lucky, the moon strays there.

"Here, *Manay*, you eat my other half – no, maybe, you shouldn't . . ." Rosa frowns at the ketchup-drowned specimen.

We're trying to play safe, as I said. We still don't know the X-ray results, the final evidence. The doctor will declare his verdict later today and, maybe, I don't have to sleep with feet next to my pillow after all. I must say, it's not all that olfactory-friendly.

"But it's too good to be left uneaten." I grab the remains of her cold burger and feed. "Don't worry, I have the constitution of a bull."

"Thick hide," she teases, while chasing her next breath.

"*Kapal-muks* –" Thick-face, meaning no shame.

I have none of that, but only when it comes to applying for continuous salary advances when times are hard. I don't pretend to be more than a small-time clerk in a Catholic college.

One of the lecturers, a strange guy who drives a new Lancer, must have smelled my poverty. He used to offer me his extra sandwich during lunch breaks. He's extremely religious and, according to campus rumour, might even be contemplating to enter the priesthood. He often prays with a discreet ring rosary around the middle finger of his right hand, yes, zealously invokes all the holy mysteries even during class hours, so I trusted him, but only for a while, because, after weeks of free sandwiches, his full generosity was revealed. On Valentine's day, he gave me a whole frozen chicken, offered me a lift, then tried to take me to the *biglang-liko*, "the sudden-turn", local euphemism for a short-time motel. It was quite a scene. I shoved the chicken's ass at his face and said, no, thank you. He never gave me presents again.

I wanted to tell the Dean, but couldn't be bothered. Besides, I really musn't offend anyone, as I'll be a long time yet in that college. I do one or two night classes each semester for a course that will probably stretch for God-knows-how-long. My teachers say I'm too smart to just be a clerk, so I should stick it out, but, believe me, my sister is even smarter. I'm sending her full-time to the same college where I work. Both our studies are paid through my salary deductions which are never enough, so I request for advances regularly. The college Treasurer, a kindly deacon, always accommodates these "loans", because he doesn't want us to quit school. My sister and I always get more than average marks.

"I think I have it." Rosa's tone is too flippant.

"But what else can you have, tell me, when you have everything, brains, beauty –"

"Ay, *Manay*, don't make fun of me now . . . what if the X-ray's bad . . . ?"

"On top of what you already have, kiddo, any extra ingredient won't hurt – it's curable after all."

"But too expensive . . . the medicines . . . check-ups . . ."

"Aw, we just have to cut down on our MacDos." I wink at

the bright billboard of great American cuisine. Beneath it, young MacLisa is still slaving away with her canned niceness.

I'm a bit jealous, really. Never had the Lisa-factor, that confident pleasantness, when I was young. And I was terrified of immaculate counters anyway. Back in our province long ago, my mother and I used to have arguments before she could force me to go to the bank and withdraw, too often, from the family's dwindling account. My hands and feet would grow cold. Stage-fright at the bank! Once I felt a few drops of wee soaking my pants as I stammered to the teller who, I must say, was never as chirpy as our Lisa.

"You never worry, no, you make light of all our worries." My sister is unusually pale.

"Worry won't earn you a centavo." I have learned that now. "You all right?" She really must eat.

"I can stop college for a while if money –"

"No, if things get bad, I'll stop, and that's the end of the discussion."

Because we always get by anyway. Like the time when our suburb had the worst ever monsoon flood and we couldn't leave the house. We halved an orange for breakfast and a sweet potato for dinner. In between, we slept, because, when you're asleep, you forget that you're hungry.

"Hoy, Rosa, you might like some fries instead or apple pie, you hardly ate, we need to have you looking fit for the doctor –"

"Worry won't earn you a –" Her retort concludes in frenzied coughing. She's hunched over her Coke, both hands over her mouth.

Times like this, I'm afraid her lungs might burst, and I won't have enough salary advances to put them together again, but this scene passes, it always does, I know, as I rush to her side of the table, rub her back, give her a napkin, hold her hand, crack a bad joke about barking in English, she likes that as she's been reading a lot on American imperialism for a Politics paper, while I sort of orate to her ear about how convinced I am that MacDo tastes okay, really, and she giggles and says, stop, you're tickling my throat even more –

"Ay, look what you've done!"

I overturned her Coke, and mine as I tried to save hers. Two plastic glasses roll and the table becomes a sweet river, and all eyes turn towards the giggling-coughing girls.

"Sorry, sorry, sorry . . ." I continue my oratorical mode, addressing my sister, the staring diners and Lisa, of course, who suddenly appears at my elbow, efficiently armed with rag and mop.

"It's all right, ma'am, I'll take care of it, it's all right . . . is she all right?"

"Rosa, Rosa . . . you okay?" I feel her shaking against me.

She's laughing and coughing into the napkin while mouthing the slogan "Coke adds life", she's after each breath in desperate pursuit, she's damp all over with cold sweat –

"Maybe, you should take her out for some air, ma'am." Lisa is fairly solicitous, helping me raise my wilted sister from her seat.

"I'm okay, I'm okay," Rosa keeps saying. The napkin falls from her hand –

On the table, the confirmation is clear, more definite than the long-awaited X-ray result.

Lisa sees it and draws back. My sister and I can only stare.

The napkin is blood-stained.

From a safe distance, Lisa looks shaken, worried. She keeps wiping her hands on the rag.

"It's all right, I'll take it out with me." I snatch the soiled napkin, but not before the diners at the next table have seen it. I hear the knowing murmurs. From the corner of my eye, I see Ms MacLisa mopping the spilled Coke off the floor with such ferocity.

# THE CURSE

"Aloe vera and five novenas for Maria Magdalena."

"We don't pray novenas for Maria Magdalena."

"But, maybe –"

"Why her?"

"Because."

"What exactly do you mean?"

The smooth scalp absorbs their altercation and six kinds of sweet-smelling herbs gathered from the riverbank. *Kulong-kugong, kadlum, verbena, artamesa* . . . she's wearing the river on her head and she'll walk out of this room of potions and incantations to the streets of Iraya, holding up her bounty and calling out those names of sweetness. Then the neighbours will come out of their houses, sniffing her trail. They will say, hoy, come over, you hawker of fragrances. But she will not stop. She's not selling. All these scents are her hair. And they will envy her, they with the black tresses.

"Maria Magdalena – *halat nguna*, are you insinuating –?"

"Dulce, Dulce, listen to me first." Pay Inyo, the village medicine man, grave-digger and corner store owner, is losing his cool authority under this dear, fat woman's unblinking scrutiny. She's reading me till the secrets of my bones, he thinks.

"So?" Her ample frame shifts impatiently on the wooden bench beside a stack of dried roots.

He feels overwhelmed under her knowing gaze, ay, and those beads of sweat just above her upper lip when she gets suspicious. He waves a hand, carving out some mute explanation in the air, and nearly knocks from the counter a jar of *turu-talinga*, those ear-shaped biscuits which are so popular among the kids. He takes out two "ears" and claps them over his own, then makes a funny face – "Hoy, you want my ears, little Eya?"

The head, subject of his healing expertise, comes alive, looks up, but only with her eyes; she must not disturb the medicine on her scalp. She laughs at the man with biscuit ears. "Yes, Pay Inyo, please, please."

"You're not tired yet, child, are you?"

A shake of the bald head – ay, to have some magic, to bump into a miracle. "Here, for being very patient. More ears in the jar . . .," he winks.

Tiya Dulce marches him away from the child, towards the sacks of rice behind the door, and whispers her accusation. "So, you're going to tell me now that this hairlessness is God's punishment of the mother, which has been inherited by her bastard daughter – *sige*, say it, say what everyone else has already said. It's been a while since I heard it – your turn now, isn't it?"

She's irresistible, he thinks, when she lectures in her

singsong. "But, Dulce, we've tried everything." He is at her mercy.

She scans his deeply browned, open face and easily finds the faint flicker of guilt in the eyes, the drop of the jaw, that obvious admission. She turns away. Once again, she hears the echo of condemnatory condolences during a funeral five years ago. Maria Magdalena, the bad woman with beautiful hair.

"You're just like them after all, Inyo."

"She became a saint when she washed His feet with perfume and her hair, you know that, so, maybe...some...some reversal of fate or something, who knows . . . ," he mutters to himself and half-collapses on a sack of rice, all his despond weighing him down. In his healing place-cum-variety store, the medicine man fails again, and he is sick at heart.

"I thought you were our friend." Tiya Dulce beckons to the child savouring the last crumbs – "We're going home, Eya, come."

The thick, gluey mixture is brusquely wiped off the tiny head. She does not mind; she's used to this. She stares at the fallen mess on the earth floor. No, she can't be a hawker of fragrances today.

But for five years since I buried her mother, I've chanted all my special prayers against evil spirits, sprinkled even my prize rooster's blood on this bare scalp, made endless offerings of my choicest dishes in the name of all growing things, concocted my best potions, but still no hair, not a stubble or a strand, or even a hint of black root somewhere. Still stubbornly naked as a clay pot's bottom. So, on her fifth year, I decide to confront this head's history, its maternal heritage, because that's the only thing I know, but Dulce, ay, my secret sweetness, is brewing up a storm.

Little Eya stoops down to play with Pay Inyo's most recent creation: six different herbs now splattered on the dark earth, quite unidentifiable in their crushed state. Just a soggy, greenish mass, divested of its magical intentions, more like carabao shit. She squats before it, tests it with her little finger, then finger to mouth – she spits, making a face. A shower of spittle on the old man's toe, curled in like the rest of him, but he does not notice.

Absorbed in one of their many arguments about the child, they've forgotten her. How we love our progeny, they who wear our every desire and despair on their prized heads.

"How much?" Tiya Dulce unpins the money kerchief from under her blouse.

"No, don't bother, please –"

"No, nothing for free, Inyo." Her usual reply for five years, yes, a little show of face, but always overtaken by poverty. Graciously, she had accepted every free treatment, until now. "I'll pay, at least for the medicine." She lays the kerchief on a candy jar and slowly counts the coins.

"Aloe vera and – five novenas for Saint Jude then? What do you think? Patron saint of lost causes, . . . isn't he?"

"Eya is not a lost cause!"

"You're really angry at me now."

"Here, three pesos – if it's not enough –"

"Why not Santa Rita –?"

"For impossible wishes?"

"Yes, impossible – I mean –"

"You want to make it worse, ha? Let me tell you this, Inyo, *sige*, lose hope and, like all the others, damn this child to eternal hairlessness, because of her poor mother's past. But in my family, we don't despair, you see. Next week, I'll see another *herbularyo* with better medicines and prayers which will be said without judgement."

"But five years, Dulce . . ."

"That's not forever."

"You're really angry at me now."

"What do you think?"

"Yes, you're very angry, I can tell."

"Take this." She forces the money into his palm. "If it's not enough, Pilar will bring you a sack of sweet potatoes –"

"Are you really that angry?"

"What do you think?"

"Ay, Dulce –"

"Trust me, I'll send Pilar over, so don't you worry –"

"But – but –"

Innocent of her history, Eya looks up at her surrogate mother and their cowed neighbour facing each other with much regret. They speak as if she can't hear, and if she can hear, as if she would never understand. But they forget that she has just eaten another pair of ears; she hears more than they can. Ay, it is these sad adults who never hear the persistent geckos in their throats, repeating the same syllables over and over again – tu-ko! – tu-ko! – tu-ko! – breaking the sweaty stupor of a summer afternoon.

Pilar reckons Pay Inyo, "the holarawnd man", likes them a lot, or her mother, more perhaps? He hasn't accepted any payment for almost five years of treating that bald thing, he doesn't mind if she and Bolodoy and sometimes Eya, of course, raid his jars of candies and biscuits, and he helps her mother dig sweet potatoes at the farm, that is, when he's not digging professionally. He's all right, this "holarawnd man". That's how he describes himself when he's boasting to the regular drinkers at his corner store after a few beers, which loosen his otherwise taciturn tongue, and after making himself more comfortable, shirt stripped off to display his "guitar".

"*Gitara*" and the title "holarawnd", by-words from an encounter long ago.

Once upon a time, thus Pay Inyo often begins this tale, a rather naive but aggressive city bum came to Iraya and had a beer too many at my store – and what happened next, children? He challenged you to a fight after some petty argument about gaming cocks, Pilar prompts him, while she and Bolodoy and Eya eat their way through the sweets at his store. They all know the event by heart now, down to its littlest detail, even the manner in which the young man posed his challenge.

"So, you wanna fight, ha?" This was punctuated by an aggressive burp, followed by a double hiccup, right at Pay Inyo's face.

"A friendly *mano-mano*, well, why not?" the old man agreed.

Enemy established then, the city relic thought. So he stripped off his shirt and began parading a well-padded chest, which rose like breasts, nipples taut like the rest of him, as he flaunted his biceps – look, real He-man, *bako*?

Not to be outdone, Pay Inyo did the same, stripped off his shirt, and strutted about. But all his drinking friends and even the curious passers-by, who decided to stay and watch the little drama, howled with laughter – he was stick-thin! A long-dried bamboo pole with clearly defined nodes, err, ribs.

With an exaggerated swagger, Pay Inyo insisted that, because this was his turf, he must set the rules of the fight, understood? Mister He-man, who was not very bright, agreed. He thought Pay Inyo was preparing for a fist fight, as he had bared his "muscles" – wasn't this the signal of ultimate aggression? He didn't know that, for the drinking crowd, it was a mere settling down ritual. Go topless in the heat and sweat out all that beer more comfortably.

"Hokay, let's see, what can you do, my boy?" the old man asked, swaying drunkenly like a frail rice-stalk.

"I can box, Cassius Clay style, wanna see, ha?" The rooster started "dancing" and throwing mock punches at his puny opponent. Everyone clapped, imagining themselves at a ringside.

"What else – ?" Pay Inyo ducked a blow.

"What do you mean?"

"Other than boxing – you work, plant, fish, what do you do?"

"We-e-ll . . ." The "dancing" lost a bit of fire.

"Yes, what else – other than 'dance'?" The crowd tittered.

"And grow breasts, yeheey!" someone added with a cat-call.

"I box . . . and . . . what else do I do . . . I take care of my body . . . see?"

"Only two jobs? Ay, *daog taka* – beat you there. Me, I'm a 'holarawnd man' – know what that means?"

"Nuh –"

A wink and a blissful gurgle. "You listen now to wisdom, boy. 'Holarawnd' means I do many things. Lots and lots. First, I do business, see? This is my own store, where I take care of all bodies – with food! And with spirits, of course – beer, gin, you name it!"

Applause all around. Everyone knew Pay Inyo as a generous soul, but a hopeless businessman who gave his poorer customers and drinking mates an endless credit line.

"And for your information, I'm an *herbularyo*, too, so I cure bodies, free them from bad spirits, those that fizzle in another way, you know –"

A circuit of chuckles.

"Then, when cure-less, I return their bodies to the earth, in order to free their good spirit this time, get me? My dear boy, I'm also a grave-digger –"

He-man stared, scratching his head, wondering how this speech would culminate.

"And you with your great chest and me, all ribs? No – *gitara*, my dear boy, this is *gitara*, pluck each rib for a note – say, you can 'dance'? Well, hear me sing –" Pay Inyo declaimed between hiccups, then broke into a plaintive serenade, strumming his bony chest up and down, up and down, while the crowd cheered and the drinkers guffawed between swigs of beer.

"So, you 'He-man', me, 'holarawnd man'. I have many jobs, boy, many jobs. And I can do more, but not enough time to enumerate all – so I beat you, see?" he said, throwing a double punch at the air.

"Yes, yes, great man Inyo – In-yo! In-yo! In-yo!" The crowd cheered some more, stamping their feet and clunking each other's beer bottles. "Another round of big gulps for Inyo, yeheeey!"

The poor He-man wilted, broad chest caving in as he stupidly stared about, then backed away. "What pathetic hicks!"

And that, children, was the famous retreat which cemented my reputation, fixed it in history, of course. Pay Inyo always ends his tale with a raised fist and a vigorous nod. Of course, his young audience readily applauds, even Pilar who is quite sceptical about the possible "embellishments" in the narrative. She agrees, however, that he is indeed the Mister Hol-arawnd of Iraya – their "all-around" man, their Jack-of-all-trades. He can do almost anything except stand up against her mother, who now orders her to bring him a sack of sweet potatoes and cassava and a bit of yam, some kind of gift or something, who knows – and choose the best ones, girl.

Now eleven years old, Pilar has not yet outgrown the two

cowlicks which rule the top of her scalp and her disposition. Cowlick. The focal point on one's crown, that spot where all hairs seem to converge. Everyone has one. But for those who have two – ay, *Dios mio*! Pilar's "two eyes of a hurricane" make for an impossibly incorrigible personality, the old folks lament. She's a natural handful, this girl who wears her hair like a boy's, neatly cropped and almost severe except for a fringe that softens her features. Occasionally, she flashes a peculiar smirk, a defiant coyness, as if she were proclaiming, "I've-a-secret-but-why-should-I-tell-you". She likes the "holarawnd man", because he cares for her mother whom she loves, but next only to Carmen, her best friend who died five years ago. No one knows this, of course. Pilar is secretive, loyal and confident, a gritty little heart that broke only once, under the guava trees where she hid her tears during the funeral. And nothing much has changed after five years – I'm your queen, always tough, don't you forget this, and you, Bolodoy, are my minister. You, Eya, well, you can be my bald slave.

She heaves the sack of tubers on her back with an economy of movement known only to those who are certain of their strength.

The kingdom is a crumbling wooden house built on a hectare of fruit trees. Balustraded steps ascend to a sagging *balkon* which leads to a massive door; it sighs when you knock, betraying the timbre of rotting wood. On the west end of the house, the large *capiz* window begins to shimmer. Its opaque shell-inlay assumes a pearl-like lustre as the house welcomes the vibrant make-over.

Amber light is kind. Lush, syrupy, spilling over warp and wear, hiding age in a languorous ooze. It is summer, five o'clock and so moist, even the leaves must be sweating.

Unknown to Eya, this is so like her dead mother's favourite afternoon that humidly stretches forever, once the perfect time for lazy baths in the river with the devoted Pilar, she who secretly guards the history of her slave whom she now orders to become an angel –

> *Salampating liya-liya*
> *Tuminugdon sa kristiya*
> *Nahiling ni Padre Biya*
> *Kuminantang alleluia –*

"*Sige na*, sing the alleluia now, Eya, c'mon – alleluia, alleluia –"

> A rocking dove
> Alights on the sacristy
> Padre Biya sees her
> She sings Alleluia

– Pilar's naughty version of the Latin "Regina", which is sung by the appointed angel during the Easter dawn celebration. Angelhood, every little girl's dream in Iraya. Ah, to be chosen as the winged darling who emerges from the *kalampuso*, a heart-shaped contraption made of pale rice-paper and wood, which opens from the top of a five-metre bamboo scaffolding. Tied to a rope around her waist, the angel is lowered from this paper heart in a dramatic descent of fairy white dress, cotton wings, a white crown of plastic flowers with fake pearls and, don't forget, the full face make-up which inspires her feeling of being as holy as a movie star.

But she is an angel who must remain floating in mid-air despite the terror in her little heart that the rope might snap or the scaffolding might collapse or that she won't be able to stand this creeping nausea, made even worse by the tight rope around her belly. The angel is afraid, but the show goes on. She releases the dove of peace, which had been shitting on her hands while they were both trapped in the heart, then sings the "Regina".

Then comes the highlight of the performance – the *Mater Dolorosa* passes by, a gothic plaster figure with her daggered heart, on a *caro* adorned with flowers. She is carried by the men directly under the angel who, in mid-flight, must lift this Blessed Mother's veil of mourning with hands folded in prayer. It has to be perfectly timed, scrupulously choreographed by the faithful, this resurrection from grief on the third day.

Yes, Pilar also dreamt of becoming an angel when she was little, but secretly. They were too poor and too busy working in the sweet potato farm. The race towards angelhood was expensive and ate up too much precious time. It meant winning a "money contest" or, kindly put, assisting the church's fund-raising project. In this worthy task, the stage mothers of the seven- to nine-year-old aspirants must compete at selling the most number of tickets in the name of their daughters. The biggest earner wins the title of "angel" – ay, what she would have given to be an angel, even just once!

But on this damp afternoon in the dreamer's kingdom, there is no competition. Pilar had outgrown her chance of divinity. The only eligible angel, of course, is the smaller girl, now tied to a rope which is precariously slung over the thickest branch of an ancient tree, and managed like a pulley from below by the queen devil and Bolodoy, her reluctant minister – yes, hang the slave!

The bastard angel is hanging from the fart-fart tree. The *atut-atut*. Earlier, Eya protested against the choice of tree whose leaves, once crushed, emit the foulest scent. This hardy and very tall creature is out of place in a yard of fragrant guavas, jackfruits, oranges, coffee and cacao. Can't be helped, as Tiya Dulce vehemently dismisses any protest against a trivial discomfort and the suggestion that the cul-

prit be chopped down. What's a bit of unpleasant smell anyway if it gives good shade in summer?

But, sister, I can do my alleluia from the jackfruit tree
instead, the would-be angel argued. It's as sturdy and not so
high up. No, only the best tree for angels like you, was the
rascal's retort. Ah, the queen bully delights in torture, of
course. She had even generously rubbed the rope around
Eya's stomach with the dreaded leaves, I bless you with this
holy fart, before the angel was hoisted up, up.

"C'mon sing, you stupid angel – why don't you sing –
alleluia, alleluia –"

"I don't think we should do this." Her brother Bolodoy,
older but much smaller in build and spirit, can't bear to look
at the little body clawing the air. "She's hurting, oh, she's
hurting, I know –"

"Aw, shut up. Just keep pulling. We'll take her higher yet –
pull!"

"Ay, sister, sister, my tummy! My tummyyyyy!" The
rope's cutting into her navel and the world is spinning.
"Take me down, take me down, *arayyyyyy!*"

Five years later, the dead woman's child is still wailing,
her cry buoyed by a sudden wind around the same yard, as
if the summer funeral never ended. But, under this generous amber light, the ripening orchard is not at all disturbed,
like the last time. The trees remain detached from this
afternoon torture, because there are preoccupations more
urgent than heeding a cry for help – like growth. The crimson coffee berries are busy brewing its flavours, the cacao
seeds are putting on their luscious white coats, the jackfruit
is blooming and the guavas are just as sweet, delectably pink
in their insides – and Pilar has not yet forgiven the child
who killed her friend. Because no one has explained the
death of Carmen, the fifteen-year-old girl-mother. Because

no one has really buried her. Because there was no resurrection from grief on the third day.

Five years ago, Pilar saw through a hole on the wall how the conspiracy unfolded, how her own mother had wrenched the hairless rat out of her friend, how the sheets and the basin of water turned red, and how the lovely Carmen grew very pale and still on a cushion of luxurious hair, the longest in the village. Then all life seemed to have gathered around the bald latecomer. And from then on, even after the village had exhausted all speculations about its unknown father, the midwife and the dead girl's then ailing mother spoke only in whispers –

We will remember only in our hearts, but this baby must not know. Best to keep the poor dear out of it, best to keep silent, then the rest of Iraya will hush its malicious murmurings. And, please, you will stay here and become her family, the new grandmother pleaded. You, Dulce, will be her new mother. And this, my father's house, is now your own home. A year later, the old woman died, and Dulce promised to love the orphan as much as her own children. But even more, even more, Pilar has always believed. Ay, Mamay has never loved more passionately.

"Brother, put me down, please, Brotheeeeeer!" The child shrieks as the rope is tugged sharply and she's jolted farther up, her back hitting the great trunk.

"I'm getting her down now, whatever you say," Bolodoy begins to loosen the rope –

"You fighting me, ha? Ha?" Pilar viciously elbows him and pulls the rope even harder.

Eya is crying and kicking about, imploring the pair below.

"You're foolish and mean and – why are you so – so –" He grasps her wrist, trying to get her hand off the rope.

"Let go! I said, let go – *lechero ka!*" She bites his hand.

"*Aray ko poo!*" He lets go and punches her – "*Lintian ka* – may the lightning strike you!"

She hits him back.

The rope breaks free and a screaming angel falls from the sky.

Thick, black eyebrows that grow towards each other, as if about to meet. No doubt about it, the child is *sarabaton* – prone to meeting spirits, that's why. And what curly lashes, and, if those eyes were open, I'd swear they're light brown, as if she were *mestiza*, but, no, she's too dark to be one – wonder who's the father. Forehead broad, its tanned smoothness extending forever, till the back of the head. Bald, thus the purple bruise is obvious. The kiss of a bad spirit.

The child moans, her breathing uneven again, as if she were chasing precious air. Pay Inyo imagines the tiny heart trying its hardest beneath the scrawny chest. He has seen birds breathe this way after a fatal blow from a slingshot.

There are several novenas at his feet. Also, some *piedra lumbre*, white medicinal stones, herbs and the ashes of *oliva* which was blessed last Palm Sunday. Among his healing implements, the old man squats to prepare the red candle and the basin with water. He scans a tattered notebook of *orasyones*, his special incantations.

He dare not look behind him. He has stopped meeting her eyes, since she called for him an hour ago, lest she betray the unspoken. But he senses her fear, as ample as herself, ascending the stairs of his vertebrae. His back is growing heavier, too heavy, it might collapse.

"Her mother died here . . ." Tiya Dulce's voice is tight; her singsong, off-key. ". . . this bed, my hands . . ."

And I buried her, he almost adds, but cups water instead, whispers it a prayer then lets it trickle back into the basin.

"But I took care of her child well . . . birth-ed her . . ." The midwife turns over a memory. "And loved her . . . I love my Eya . . . she's mine now, you know . . ."

"Mamay . . ." Pilar whispers behind the door. Her brother echoes her tone, hungry for reassurance.

"Just stay there, both of you . . ." she tries to regain the old authority, the scolding attitude, but fails. "It will be all right, children . . . it will be . . ."

"Let them in. I need help," says the medicine man. His dolorous voice is so deep, as if drawn from his toes. "Come in, Pilar, Bolodoy . . . sit with me, you, too, Dulce . . . I need help."

Pilar sees her, so pale, even her scalp is pale, except for that purple. Her gaze must not leave that frail rise and fall, lest it stops – see, she's alive, she's alive, she's alive, she chants to herself, trying to echo the rhythm of the patient's breathing. Of course, the holarawnd man can do everything, yes, make her better again – but what to tell him now? Ay, Bolodoy hit me, so I hit back, then – hush, not a word, no, don't you tell on us, Bolodoy. Yes, it's bad spirits, Pay Inyo, they're up to their tricks, they've always been, you said, keeping her hair from growing like that, you know, because they don't want her to be beautiful like her mother, and, Mamay, we were just playing and she climbed the fart-fart tree, I told her not to, Bolodoy, too, we told her, but up she went, she went and fell, just like that, when the bad spirits pushed her –

"Where did you play this afternoon?" Pay Inyo has lighted the red candle.

"Yard," Bolodoy mumbles.

"Which part?" He lets the candle wax drip on the water.

A ripples of wishes.

"Under the *atut-atut* and she climbed up and fell and that's why –"

"How could you let her, girl, you're the older one, you're supposed to take care of her, you stupid – you should have –" The surrogate mother is passing on a five-year-old guilt, that ultimate terror, so excruciating, it drives us to love. "My Eya, my poor child . . . my darling . . ."

"Hush, Dulce, please – how, Pilar? How did it happen?" He scrutinises the wax hardening on the water, then murmurs an incantation. A ripple of fears.

"Just fell."

"Did you see anything unusual around that tree? Any strange mounds of earth or some hovering insect, anything?"

"No." Both children answer hastily.

The candle splutters a faint protest.

"This, seen anything like this?" The medicine man points to the red wax floating on the water. In the candlelight, a splatter of coagulated blood or a red raft, oddly shaped –

"The spirit, Dulce. Here, see this. It's a female spirit, a young female spirit, a girl . . ."

Bolodoy clutches his sister's hand, uttering a choked cry.

Pilar stares at the solid blob of red on the basin, what girl, it's only wax, there's no girl, what's all the fuss, she's all right, don't be stupid, watch her chest, she'll be all right, she's alive, she's alive, she's –

The rise and fall halts, abandoning the imposed rhythm, and the purple slowly spreads, the scalp breaking into sweat –

Ay, my cruel God! Swallowing his despair, the holarawnd man begins to chant all the *orasyones* that he can remember, desperately leafing through his novenas, trying to find that lost magic, that stingy miracle, willing the heavens to open, to grant that secret, elusive grace, so small a plea, Saint Jude, *tabi man*, Santa Rita, have mercy on us!

# THE LONG SIESTA
# AS A LANGUAGE PRIMER

I, too, can love you
in my dialect, you know,
punctuated with cicadas
and their eternal afternoons:
*"Mahal kita, mahal kita."**

---

* Filipino for "I love you, I love you". Crooned by fourteen-year-old Che-che to her foreigner b.f. (boyfriend) Mr Shoji X, a fifty-year-old paper magnate with a secret logging concession in Palawan in the southern Philippines. Crooned with feeling – *kilig* to the bone he was* – at a five-star hotel suite on a long, hot afternoon, while he was dressing up to catch his plane back to X-landia.

---

* *Kilig*. Filipino for "quiver". Quiver to the bone. Street idiom meaning "very excited". Mr Shoji X was *kilig* to the bone, Che-che thought, as she watched her baby lips open and close over the syl-

lables of native endearment, *"mahal kita, mahal kita"*, while he zipped up his pants. Che-che was humouring her b.f., who is truly *madatung\**, for a bigger tip.

---

\* Full of cash; rich. Local idiom referring to the well-heeled. Mr Shoji X, genuinely *madatung* and generous, too, always wore the most expensive Ballys. Scored in Europe. Che-che had a discerning eye. Not new to her trade, two years in business, and she was well trained. Aunty Dearest taught her to "look at the shoes, dearie, the shoes". This beloved *bugaw\** was an expert. She could tell if the sole was not leather.

---

\* Term for "pimp". Aunty Dearest had literally saved the girl from starvation, so the story runs around Ermita's grapevine. She came to Manila after a devastating typhoon in her province. The storm had destroyed their hut after it claimed her mother's life. Thank god, Aunty Dearest played surrogate Mama to the poor girl after she had found her scavenging in the dump beside Manila Bay. What tragic waste! Too beautiful to die among the garbage. It broke her heart, Aunty Dearest said. We must help each other, dear. She bought her three Big Macs the first time they met. The *bugaw* was Che-che's *kababayan\** after all.

---

\* From the root word *"bayan"* meaning "province". Term addressed to one who comes from the same province as the speaker. Aunty Dearest's and Che-che's *bayan* is Laguna, not famous for its strong typhoons unlike other parts of the Philippines. But two years ago, the disaster struck. Che-che had to move to Manila, met her *kababayan*, and the rest is history. Che-che is naturally *ma-L\**, her colleagues believe, that's why she has so many diehard b.f.'s.

---

\* A shortened version of *"malibog"*. Literally means "with very active libido"; a way of saying "very horny". "Che-che is *ma-L*", so the *chismis\** goes among the young wards of Aunty Dearest. Che-che doesn't mind though. Best advertisement, she says.

* Meaning "gossip". Derives from Spanish. Che-che doesn't make *chismis*. She is not *chismosa*. Waste of time. Use mouth for profitable venture instead. But business that afternoon was not all that profitable. Her favourite b.f. was a disappointment, despite the fact that he is *madatung* and visits the Philippines every month, and lives in five-star hotels. He was not himself that afternoon. Her *suki*\* was losing his golden touch.

* Term for "regular customer". The *suki* of all *suki*, this Mr Shoji X, Che-che winked conspiratorially at the bellboy in the lift. Generous, too, except this time when he had rushed out of their suite without handing her the usual tip. Got the standard pay, of course, but not the fat tip. He was running late, so he forgot. I'm just making *habol*\* after my dues, you know, Che-che had to explain to the prim woman at the reception desk, as she tried to chase after him.

* Literally means "to run after". But Che-che had missed her b.f. by just a minute. The taxi limousine was now rolling down the exit ramp and reception was detaining her with questions. All because he was so *praning*\* about losing face – we must never take the lift together, he had said. Look what happened now.

* Filipino camp version of "paranoid". Che-che was also getting *praning* as several front-of-house staff gathered around her, while the hotel security guard gripped her arms to keep her from making *habol* after the disappearing tail of the limousine. They were going to call the cops, because she was not legal. Imagine, Mr Shoji X had also forgotten to pay the desk fee, *putang ina*!\*

* Meaning "whore Mama!" You bad-mouthing me? The prim receptionist's tone was deadly. Of course not! They never remember this face – me, a *suki* of this hotel, too! She handed her purse to the *putang inang* receptionist. Haay, there goes my *merienda*\*, Che-che sighed.

* Refers to an afternoon snack. After long *siesta*, no *merienda*, Che-che glowered at the setting sun of Manila Bay while clutching her empty purse. Above, the pink trail of a 747 was just beginning to crumble.

# THE KISSING

Gingered chicken in green papayas, smoth-
ered with coconut milk, never fails to keep the tongue moist
long after the meal is over. So does slightly burnt sugar
lodged at the roof of the mouth, melting with infinite slow-
ness. The acrid sweetness teaches the tongue not to forget.
Such is the taste of a kiss at the front door, when one foot
must already seek the first step down, while the heart
remains on a plate at the head of the table. Especially when
it's the first and last kiss, especially when it's first love.

Manolito the cook was sixteen when he was forced to say
goodbye to her. He was a good cook, a very heartbroken
good cook one summer night in Iraya when the master
found out that the presumptuous son of a peasant had kissed
Clarita, his beloved only daughter. Don Miguel Balaguer
had witnessed the unforgivable insolence in his own house by
the light of the candelabra at his own table. The crime took
place after he had enjoyed a generous helping of the cook's
famous *linupak* special, right after he loosened his belt to let

his stomach breathe. Clarita was at the head of the table, as she always was, and he had just gone to the *balkon* to light his final cigar of the day when that *puñeta* did it – I will not have a rapist for a cook. No, not even if he's the best cook in the planet!

One hand to his chest, as if missing his heart, and the other rubbing his lips over and over again, Manolito sat at the edge of his bamboo bed, hardly aware of his bruises. He had almost done it in that shadowed dining room, finally mustered enough courage to seek those lips behind the flickering candles, those always smiling lips of his *Señorita*. Lips which flaunted the crimson sheen of the *tambis* berry, which grew even more fiery by the light of eighteen tongues of flame. And always that slight lift at the corners of the mouth, there with a hint of a dimple, every time he served his meal offerings. And what about the dark brown eyes, ay, those tamarind-seed eyes, which perpetually glanced down to her left, and unobtrusively surveyed every wonder that he had seasoned with his own hands. Manolito made sure that her favourite dishes were always meticulously arranged to her left, so she could check that the *cosido* soup clouded over in a just-right way, that the green papayas in the chicken dish were still firm but tender to the bite and that the fern salad was not drowned by too much lemon, but still kept its vibrant green curlicues. Ay, doesn't her hair curl that way at the ends!

Manolito ran his hand over the bamboo bed that was now polished by his back, by all his nightly tossing and turning for the past six months, sometimes till the cock's first crow. He should have known that he was doomed from that night he came to cook for the Villa Clarita, from the minute he stepped into the *comidor*, the only room that had no need of electric light. Instead, candles lit, as if for an eternal wake, at the head of the long, wooden table – ay, he should have been forewarned! But, no, bearing the steaming pork stew, his first accomplishment on the job, into the grand dining room, he was not at all deterred by the sight which met him. He charged headlong to his undoing.

The walls were alive with shadows flung from the dining table which was a dark hardwood carved with *cadena de amor* around the edges. One shadow, bent by a hill-on-her-back, moved about armed with a fly swatter – Yaya Conching, housekeeper and nanny to the *Señorita*, as Manolito was to later understand. The corpulent Don Miguel, on the other hand, was fairly still except when he puffed his appetiser. His shadow evoked an immense *capre*, the cigar-smoking ghost which lived in old *balete* trees. But the new cook was hardly impressed. It was the third shadow, rigid and rectangular behind the head chair, that would eventually break his heart.

"Hoy, quick, young man, or that stew will get cold," Yaya Conching beckoned him. "Don Miguel, this is Manolito, our new cook."

The master ignored the earnest boy at his elbow though his once fine patrician nose, grown bulbous from too many years of wine and rich food, twitched slightly. The stew's fragrant bay-leaf sauce never failed to achieve its desired effect.

"No, no, not here. There, put that over there, close to our Clarita. Offer it to your *Señorita* first." The old woman with the hill-on-her-back waved at him with the fly swatter. Manolito could only stand and gape.

Yaya Conching directed him towards the head of the table where the candelabra were clustered, where one long, still shadow bloomed like a headstone, and where she sat with her eternal half-smile. Also framed in hardwood with the *cadena de amor* motif was a painting of the most beautiful girl in the world. It – she – was propped on the *cabisera*, the head-of-the-house dining chair, the most-important-person chair, the chair that would from then on haunt Manolito's dreams. Clarita Balaguer at the head of the table.

"Are you sure you got the right one for the job, ha, Conching?"

"Ay, of course, *Señor*, of course, he's the son of our most reliable cook, the one who died last year, and her boy's the best cook in Iraya now, so I hear – hoy, *torpe*, I said the stew goes beside *Señorita* Clarita – hoy!"

I have almost repeated history, Manolito sighed into his hands that smelled of spices and despair. He gazed at the packed bag at his feet. Zipped up and ready to go, how lost it looks, as if aware that its owner was just a poor servant who had almost kissed the ghost of his dead mistress. Yes, a silly village boy who had pantomimed the past – a long time ago, an American Peace Corps volunteer had also stolen a kiss from Clarita's mother. In that same *comidor*, the very much alive *Señora* Balaguer had tasted something sweeter than dessert, so she left her husband and baby for that white man, the slut! And the Don never recovered – never, never, the village drunk had hiccupped the tale into Manolito's ears.

Picking up his bag, Manolito vowed never to recover from the charms which seasoned his cooking with such fervour, allowing him to create the most flavoursome *paella*, the perfectly stuffed *bangus*, the tenderest *pochero* and his extraordinary boiled rice made fragrant by pandan leaves which he himself grew with nightly incantations of devotion. And, of course, his *linupak* special in its richest blend of sticky yams, young coconut meat, roasted peanuts, palm sugar, fresh carabao milk and the secret beating of his heart.

"What are you muttering about, ha?" Yaya Conching wondered at Manolito's odd style of preparing his *linupak*, the way he whispered to each ingredient before pounding it in the huge wooden mortar. "You crazy?"

The young cook only tossed back his head in answer, clearing the thick fringe off his brow.

"Talking to yourself again, of course." Yaya Conching was both curious and amused. "So, what's your secret?" She suspected some furtive sorcery in all this whispering. But definitely good magic, what with Don Miguel's delight over his excellent cooking. A true genius, this boy – and so young, too. "Hoy, *baya*, what spell are you invoking this time, ha?"

The task was getting more strenuous, almost backbreaking, as the sweet mixture became a paste so thick, the heavy pestle nearly stuck to the mortar. But he did not wish to rest; he felt strong. He smiled with secret pleasure at the sticky blend clinging to his pestle, which he raised with an exultant heave, all the while luxuriating in the delicious broadening of his shoulders and arms, the tightening of his ribs which held back all the longings of the heart.

"*Padaba, padaba, padaba*... beloved, beloved, beloved..." Such was his chant to each yam, to the slivers of coconut meat, to every ingredient of this special dessert, wooing each one to be in its best flavour for his Clarita, the mistress of the house. She who will be forever fifteen in that portrait at the head of the table.

"Yes, you're mad, mad indeed," Yaya Conching tut-tutted back to her chores, seeing that the young hero of the pestle-and-mortar was not going to let her in on his culinary secrets.

No madder than you or Don Miguel or this house that believes its daughter is alive, is still sitting at the head of the table as she had always done since her mother abandoned her for America – sacked, packed and ready to fly, Manolito could not help but recount to himself the story which had become his own. *The kissing*, the whole of Iraya referred to it, the tragedy of the kissing. Caught in the act after dessert. The wild Asuncion and the dashing *Amerikano*, and the cuckolded Don who was even more devastated when his Clarita died of tuberculosis three years ago.

Manolito took one last look at his cramped room and the bamboo bed, the only one that knew his fever. But I am no American and I have nowhere to fly to. And, of course, my beloved – even if she loves me, too, or even if she loves my cooking, so that she almost loves me, too – would never be able to walk out of her father's canvas sitting at the head of the table. And, worse, our lips never touched. I only *nearly* kissed her.

What dish could make the dead eat again, Manolito had asked as he stirred the chicken and papaya into the coconut milk that night of the alleged crime of passion. What flavour would make a portrait come alive, he wondered while squeezing green lemons into the *cosido* soup as if seeking inspiration from its milky rice-wash. What culinary spectacle would move those berry lips to open so she could partake of my love. Manolito felt the heat from the stove flushing his face, spreading to his breast and settling in his loins which burned like his hot *ensaladas*.

Tenderly spooning his *linupak* special into a big bowl, he thought of the hundreds of "beloveds" he had uttered before the pestle and mortar that afternoon as he worked every muscle in order to prepare this dessert. Yes, hundreds of failed endearments, because the *Señorita* will never be able to know the taste of my affection. So good was the dish that Don Miguel praised it in one of the rare moments when he addressed his cook. So good, it could even make me forget my name, he belched extravagantly before retiring to the *balkon* for his last cigar.

So good, it will even make you forget that you're dead, Clarita, Manolito whispered as he offered her the bowl which held the remains of his one hundred endearments. Dinner was over and only a few candles were left spluttering in their tiny flames. Manolito had never felt so bold. He had never come this close to her portrait before, never gone past the flickering candles that fenced her, never faced her with this much courage. Just the two of them now and their shadows, his own merging with the rigid, rectangular headstone on the wall. But she would not look at him, her eyes still gazing down to the left as if waiting for another miracle from his stove, as if searching for one more vow of love. And with lips half-smiling as if eternally pleasured, or perhaps amused by her cook's exertions to outdo himself each day for her sake. Seeing her this close, Manolito was beside himself with desire.

But you have to know it, taste it, this thing that has seasoned the most fervent courtship of all, *Señorita*, this fire in the stove, yes, its heat which would shame even the hottest spice in the pantry – please, let me tell it to your mouth. Mad Manolito then scooped some *linupak* with his forefinger and sucked it, after which he intoned his hundred endearments to her lips. So good, beloved, it will even make you forget that you're dead.

The kissing, the kissing, Don Miguel screamed as he pummelled the startled lover with his fists, until, like a tired mother, Yaya Conching hushed him down into weeping. Get out of my house, American bastard, the cigar-smoking shadow cried, shrinking into his chair, while the other shadow with the hill-on-her-back gathered the broken man. Thirteen years ago, Don Miguel did not lay a finger on his wife's lover who was two heads taller than him. He had remained civil. Please, get out of my house – and take the whore with you.

Saying goodbye to his kitchen, Manolito tried to locate the seat of the ache, where the cut flesh seemed seared by the juice of green lemons rolled in salt. Is it in the lips, that unhealable gash of the face, that wound for food, speech and tender things? Must be in a forgotten slit in the heart, drawn by God from our birth, that which we remember only at sixteen, the most intimate cut. Or, perhaps, it rests in the smarting eye of the loin, wide awake at night and weeping. The sun in my house must not rise on your face, you hear? The Don had made this clear to him. I want you out of here tonight, *ora mismo*!

It was nearly midnight when Manolito shuffled through his kingdom. Before the stove, he let his bag fall to his feet – ay, *Madre*, what a fate! But he could not imagine life without cooking for the *Señorita*. There were only two things in this world that he could do well, cook and love, and tomorrow both of these would be impossible. For the first time since the almost-kissing a few hours ago, he realised that, away from this kitchen and Clarita, he would be useless.

If only I had really kissed her. At least, I would have something to take away with me. But he could perhaps leave with the taste of the actual kissing and the aftertaste of history, why not?

Tiptoeing towards the dining table, he felt again the queer sensation around his lips, this time with renewed elation. The *comidor* was a tomb. The candles had died and the headstone shadow had been swallowed by the walls. The cook scanned the darkness with his hands as if brushing away all the cobwebs that had buried an old story. I know she's been waiting ever since dessert, after the Don had withdrawn to the *balkon* for his cigar. Suddenly I am strong and tall, very tall, two heads taller than the master of this house. And I will prove him right in his accusation.

As a carved tendril of the *cadena de amor* grazed his hips, Manolito shivered with anticipation. Reaching out, he found the arm of the head chair – this is it, the *cabisera*! Raising a hand with utmost care, lest he knock down his beloved, he attempted to braille her features. Those lips, those berry lips, his fingers tingled in their frantic search . . . air . . . nothing but air? What – where – wrong chair?

Like the earnest "it" in a blind man's buff, Manolito circled the table, arms outstretched – left? Gone? With the ghost of her mother and the American. Also after dessert, without even tasting my famous *linupak* special, crooned into perfection by a hundred endearments – and, *santissima*, not a soul knew, much less cared. Ay, the tragedy of the kissing is mine, mine alone, Manolito sank into the empty chair at the head of the table and wept.

The next day, with a big ache in the hill-on-her-back, Yaya Conching had to cook dinner. As a side-dish to the leftover chicken and papaya of the night before, she opted for some banana heart in a hot *ensalada*. Running the tap on the heart, she kept seeing the lost look on the boy's face as he dragged his feet to the door. He had left after midnight, a somnambulist whispering some incantation which sounded strangely like the spell that he uttered over the pestle and mortar – I say, brilliant cook, though a trifle crazy, but, haay, *salamat sa Dios*, now it's all over. And it was about time that the master returned that portrait to its proper place in the sitting room. All in a night's work that sudden enlightenment, a return to sanity at last. What blessing, this second kissing, she nodded to the banana heart on the wooden board – but poor Manolito. Knife poised before the magenta velveteen skin, she wished him luck. Ay, he'll find another job soon, silly kid. A pity though, he was such a good cook, she sighed, cutting the heart in half.

# THE REVIEW

Eighty-year-old May pegs the blanket on the line; the writer has her first coffee. Eleven o'clock. May breathes them in. At last, clean chrysanthemums, pink and white. The writer sips her instant brew – where's the fucking thing? She thumbs through three Saturday papers.

"Each time I reap the last wash from the line, I bury my dead a little bit more," May murmurs the ending of the writer's first book as she stoops to pick up the laundry basket. When she first read it, she imagined that it was specially written for her, handed to her like a gift. And that, since then, she has always held its final words in her hands, cupped like a chalice. Do not clutch; let them breathe. "Never hidden like soiled clothes, but washed and hung out to dry. Air it, air it."

The writer can't find it – for God's sake, half a year now after her wretched book came out! Don't you bank on him, a friend had cautioned her. At the launch, a critic said he was interested to review her first book. She was thrilled. She even asked him over for coffee – bloody awful coffee! Perfect punctuation for another week's futile wait.

The futility of soiled retro shirt and pants, with pink and white hearts, and the red socks, his fire-socks. So today, May washed them finally along with the blanket. During the last days at the hospital, her only son Elmer preferred to use his own things; he even asked for his "retro stuff", complete with a belt of crystals. If one must go, let it be in style. A New Ager swaddled in a pink and white chrysanthemum blanket, freshly ironed and Cold-Power scented. Beat that. But when he was born, she had wrapped him in plain blue. Well, I'm in my floral phase, Mum, pink floral, he whispered, laughing and coughing painfully all at once, after she told him about her "ancient" colour coding. Between giggles, his face paled, contorted into a white scowl, then his body clutched itself into a foetus. He wishes to return to me, she thought holding him, helping him find his next breath among the pink and white chrysanthemums which inevitably bloomed into wet, yellow patches.

The writer scans the newspaper. Something on Margaret Atwood here, one on Michael Ondaatje, a bit on Linda Jaivin and a long one on Gail Jones . . . Rosario Diaz, where are you? Diaz, Diaz – Diaz who? The writer manages a self-deprecating chuckle as she scours even the fine print at the edges. Nothing.

"The resurrection of nothing." Oh, yes, the book's first chapter. What unhinged her, May remembers now as she goes inside the house. "Doing the laundry is a vain act when we think we can wash them clean, free of history – but how to resurrect the past nonentity of a lover's dress, once merely merchandise in a shop window. As yet clean and uninhabited, no ghost of limbs . . ." May recalls her first unbridled grief upon reading that first page.

It begins after a war, peacetime, as the writer puts it iron-
ically, May reckons now while returning the extra pegs to
the cupboard. Every day, a shell-shocked guerilla washes the
dress of his missing wife in the river. He found her blue
shift, bloodied and mouldy, three months after she disappeared. "This punishment of hands, this tenderest frenzy
of knuckle against knuckle, the marked cloth between . . .
all hoping they come out clean . . ."

May sensed the book was written for her, even if Esther,
her hairdresser with whom she shared the novel, kindly
observed that May's own story was not really as bad.
Australia is not at war, lucky for us, and – But grief is grief
in whatever country, in whatever time, May retorted, cut to
the quick. Esther didn't know then that his blanket and
retro ensemble, stained with sweat and urine, were still in
the closet; May could not bear to wash them. I'm not in a
grief competition, Esther. Her hairdresser apologised and
made her a cup of tea.

Earl Grey or English Breakfast? Ah, a big decision, of
course – better than this shitty coffee! Here in Australia, the
writer learned how to swear, yes, sweet release! Fucking critic and your bloody empty promise – but he didn't really
promise, did he? Fucking wog writer, behave yourself!
Remember, this country does not owe you, a Juana-come-
lately, anything, she used to remind herself when a poem or
a short story was returned with a rejection slip. But, please,
couldn't it be different now after a major publication? Well,
who decides what's major – you, wog?

I might be presuming too much, May sighs to herself,
putting the kettle on. Last month, while retrieving her laundry, she was seized by a desire to write to her. My dear,
would you like to come for afternoon tea? I make the best
treacle scones in my street – I just want you to know I cried

myself to sleep with your book and my son's chrysanthemums. You see, I used to sleep with his blanket. Would dinner suit you instead? I don't know any Philippines dishes, but I have an Asian cookbook that I've been wanting to try . . . silly old woman, she censured herself then. Even the urge to let her hairdresser in on the plan was eventually tamed.

May has never acted on this plan since its conception, though at times she thought she might. Especially that night when she stopped using the blanket, then when she hid it in the closet along with his dirty clothes, or the day she began sorting out his things for St Vincent's, and early this morning when she decided to finally wash the remnants of those last three weeks at the hospital. I could write her tonight or tomorrow or right now, why not, May debates over a cup of tea. My dear, unlike your poor soldier, I only washed them once today, a year after the funeral. Strange, I did not even cry. I have stopped fretting about stains – NapiSan makes them extra clean, you know, like freshly laundered diapers.

"Similarly, the idea of a man washing his dead wife's dress every day, in order to remove its bloodstains and thus exorcise his loss, is both poignant and sinister. Diaz's story –" The writer is saved from her bitter musings. At last, ay, *salamat sa Dios*, thank god. On the last page of the Saturday *Herald's* review section and at the tail-end of the article on a "remarkable" collection of stories on death by another writer, "a brilliant" young Australian, the long awaited acknowledgement of her work is found. "Diaz's novel is ambitious; sadly, its emotional prose does not live up to its aspiration. This writer, who hails from Southern Philippines, could learn from the austere, unsentimental . . ."

The resurrection of nothing – the first line of her book was a blur as the writer searched for the supposedly excessive lines, the soppy turns of phrase. Her eyes felt hot as, pen in hand, she marked all those that might need amputating. Fuck you, critic, fuck you, book. In Australia, she learned how to swear; but, in moderate Australia, she must also learn how to geld her verbal outbursts. Fuck, why was I born in a land of big emotions?

Twelve o'clock. The writer and May are both having tea, each with a copy of the book. The writer pores over it; she is crying. May closes hers, finally. For the first time in twelve months, her eyes feel clean, as if newly washed, and really dry.

# PINA AND THE
FLYING CROSS

When Grandmother-in-the-knees saw her first plane, she crossed herself several times and sang the "*Te Deum*". She mistook the American fighter for a flying cross. It was the end of World War II and, in the small village of faraway Iraya somewhere in the north of the Philippines, everyone was waiting for a miracle. *Salvacion* from the retreating Japanese army, but not in the sense that the young pilot from Tennessee understood as he gawked through binoculars at the crowd of kneeling natives and flew on, feeling good and big and strong and as spiritually airborne as a white god.

The drone of the flying cross was sweeter than any "*Te Deum*", Grandmother-in-the-knees thought and everyone agreed as they rose from their prostrate stupor. And did you see that smoke? *Hesusmaryahosep*! A flying, burning cross! It's a sign! A sure sign from heaven that the war is really over! We should tell Padre Biya at once. We should have a thanksgiving mass – no, two masses, don't you think so? Oh, I can die now! He has revealed himself to me. We must be the chosen ones, Lola Conching, don't you think so? Grandmother-in-the-knees was trembling as she brushed the red earth from her homesewn *saya*, while the others waited for an answer. She was the oldest among the crowd of women who saw the flying cross. She should testify to the parish priest – the *Santo Cristo* was revealed to a group of women, imagine!

Grandmother-in-the-knees began to weep quietly. The women gathered around her, making noises about her being as overcome as they were, but that she was not very healthy, and each one offered to take her home, while reminding her of a godly responsibility. Speak with Padre Biya as soon as possible, she must!

"I'll take her home myself." Pina hugged her great-grandmother's legs protectively, her solemn eyes not missing the now arched brows of the beatified crowd.

Everyone had forgotten her. Ay, yes. The holy cross was revealed to a group of women – and a young girl, too? Pina, Lola Conching's six-year-old great-granddaughter, was very lucky indeed. To be so privileged at such a tender age, what blessing! All the women wished they had their daughters with them.

"So, you saw it, too, Pina, ha?"

"Yes. And it was not only burning. It also had eyes of fire." Pina had taken a good look at the American fighter, while all the women bowed their heads in prayer. She had seen the plane's glass windows catching the noon-day sun. Ay, *baya*, burning so, such a gaze could have scorched the bamboo hedge lining the road.

"Yes, it had eyes." Pina hugged her grandmother's legs tighter.

There was a chiding hush in the crowd. Even Grandmother-in-the-knees choked between tears and censure.

"I saw them. The eyes made it look like a giant dragonfly," Pina whispered conspiratorially.

The women could not believe their ears. They shook their heads vigorously, as though to dislodge the child's voice from their hallowed selves, while staring at the hopeless matriarch. Do something! Such blasphemy!

One of the women, Manay Elsa, came forward and held Pina roughly by the arm. "A cross does not have eyes."

"But I saw them, Grandmother-in-the-knees. Huge burning eyes."

Lola Conching had resumed her halted tears, but, this time, not because of deep emotion inspired by the beatific vision, but of embarrassed frustration. Ay, this beloved great-granddaughter of mine who keeps calling me Grandmother-in-the-knees. Yes, it's our way of distinguishing a great-grandmother like me from an ordinary grandmother, but to address me in such formal terms makes the neighbours look at us strangely. And now this? A dragonfly? Did you hear that? A dragonfly with eyes of fire? Ay, *baya*, my six-year-old cross, this little unbeliever of my Calvary! The old woman's tears ran down her cheeks and fell on Pina's hair.

"Stop raining on me, Grandmother-in-the-knees – please?" The girl tugged at her skirt.

*Atrebida!* Manay Elsa caught her breath at such insolence – had she been my daughter – ! Everyone waited for the old woman to do something, but she was not one to scold her children or her grandchildren or her great-grandchildren in public. Fair woman that she was, she believed in meting out punishment or sermon behind closed doors with only the culprit in attendance. Besides, this littlest monkey of a great-granddaughter was her favourite.

"We're going home. I'll see Padre Biya this afternoon, I promise."

The women huddled close, like hurt orphans. Lola Conching is walking away, just like that? Without even consulting them about what to say to Padre Biya, without even asking any of them to come along? But it must have escaped her mind, what with that brat. She's a strange one, isn't she? Always playing alone or following her great-grandmother around. That's what happens when a child doesn't even know who her father is – now, haven't you heard? What ignorance! That's why the mother never returned here after she left the child with Lola Conching years ago. Even her grandmother, the other one – I mean, Lola Conching's daughter, of course – hardly comes for a visit. Ay, that brat's mother was something else, you better believe me. I'd say, loose as a skirt missing its elastic.

Together, the women wove tales about Pina and her absent unwed mother, all along worrying whether Lola Conching would remember her task to see Padre Biya and whether she would give all their good names to their *Cura Paroco*. But he must know that the *Santo Cristo* was revealed to Elsa Chavez, Maria Belmonte, Asuncion Coronel, etc., etc. . . . he must!

That late afternoon, right after the mass which was very well attended, as the makeshift church had just begun holding the occasional service after the Japanese retreat, the women gathered around Grandmother-in-the-knees and, of course, Pina again. So what will you do now, Lola Conching? There's Padre Biya blessing the children. Go on, please, now's our chance. But perhaps, we should come along and talk to him, too. And, perhaps, you shouldn't take Pina with you, don't you think so? But the girl held on tightly to her great-grandmother's skirt as they advanced towards the altar where the ancient *Cura Paroco* was just blessing a crippled little boy.

"Hoy, Inggo," Pina yelled to the boy, "We just saw a giant dragonfly with a smoking tail and eyes on fire!"

The women stopped on their tracks, the children and Padre Biya stared, and the whole church fell silent. For a small and frail girl of six, Pina had such a deep bass, the other kids often teased her that, soon, she might even grow a moustache.

"So, a giant dragonfly . . . how interesting . . ." the priest chuckled above the sudden protesting buzz of the women.

"Padre, it was a cross that we saw – a flying cross," Manay Elsa solemnly announced as she walked towards the priest, sharply elbowing Pina on her way.

*Talaga*? Really, now? A crowd suddenly engulfed the confused priest and the enraptured storyteller. Her arms flew in the air as she described how the heavens opened and revealed the sky-cruising apparition to us women, us women, and don't you forget that. Lucky you, Manay Elsa. Ay, my heart just soared and soared with it, mind you. Went this way and that with the *Santo Cristo* which even left a trail of incense in the sky. *Hesusmaryahosep*, a miracle! Tell us, tell us more. Did it have the marks of Calvary, the nail holes, the blood? How exactly did it fly, float, or – zoom above your heads? Ay, Padre, this is a sign, I'm sure, the war is truly over. Over! Hoy, let's all visit the place where you saw it. Pay our respects, of course! That would be sacred ground now. *Dios ko po*, if I just lay my bad back there, perhaps, well, you never know . . .

Looking at his crippled left leg with hope, Inggo was torn between believing in miracles and enjoying a tale about giant dragonflies that blew smoke from their behinds. He felt a bit sorry for his best friend. Even her deep, indignant bass was no match against the loud chorus of the faithful.

"How could they tell? They didn't look at it hard or long enough, but I did. Really stared till it disappeared." Pina dragged him to one of the pews away from the impassioned throng.

"We-ell . . ." Inggo rubbed his leg which, he reminded himself, still hurt every night.

"Believe me, its eyes were a deep yellow. Blazing, I tell you!"

"Could be the sun from heaven – but eyes . . . *sigurado ka* – you sure?"

"Wait a minute, you don't believe me either, do you?"

"Uhmm . . ." Inggo limped back towards the crowd.

So everyone won't listen to me, Pina stamped her foot. Grandmother-in-the-knees, who's just now confirming Manay Elsa's story, and even my one and only friend. Traitor! She wanted to call out to his hunched frame. Wasn't I the one who ran back here to get some help when you fell from that tree, while we were on a lookout for the advancing Japanese? Wasn't it Grandmother-in-the-knees who massaged your leg every day so you could walk again? Why don't you call that a miracle, too?

". . . So we fell on our knees . . ."

"With our hearts overflowing with great joy . . ."

"As we prayed and wept . . ."

"While Lola Conching sang the '*Te Deum*' –"

"NOW, WE CAN HEAR IT CLEARLY!"

*Hesusmaryahosep*! Story caught in their throats, the women couldn't believe what they saw – Pina was shouting from the altar table! The altar table, of all places! She had climbed onto it and stepped on it – stepped on it, *por Dios y por Santo*! Desecrated the holy mantle, only ever touched by Jesus' body and blood, with her dirty feet – Grandmother-in-the-knees nearly fainted. The old priest was red in the face with – was it utmost concern for a lost sheep or rage at this damned boldness? The parishioners wondered how Iraya could have borne a little devil. And Inggo was absolutely scared for his silly, silly friend.

"Get off the altar of God, my child." The priest's voice quavered with painful control.

"Pina, my Pina, how could you . . . ?" Grandmother-in-the-knees was hot and cold all at once with humiliation and fear for her great-granddaughter's soul.

"So now we can hear it clearly. You were all on your knees with heads bowed in prayer – and not looking up, remember? – while I stared long and hard at the dragonfly. Ay, what a giant! It even buzzed, strangely though. Engggggg-chug-chug-chug-chug-enggggggg . . ." Pina droned while making flying motions with her arms on the table of God.

There was a brief silence after the little dramatisation. It was Padre Biya who first came out of the crowd's stupor, he who understood what the vision in question actually was. The old priest approached the altar, arms held out, coaxing Pina to come down. Haay, but what a disappointing revelation. We need real epiphanies, yes, miracles, Lord, especially at the end of a war.

"But why believe her? She's her mother's child, or have you forgotten?" Manay Elsa spat out the bitterness that must have come from aborted sainthood. Last night, she had dreamt of the shepherd children of Fatima, which inspired the thought that God loves poor village folk more than the rest of the world.

"In her stupid head, Pina braids lies the way her mother did. Remember the dreamer who fancied that all the men of Iraya were in love with her at one time?"

"You're talking about my family, Elsa." Stung to the heart, Grandmother-in-the-knees accosted the gossip in no time.

"Now, now, ladies, there's no reason to fight . . ."

"And why not, Padre?" Pina sat on the altar, cross-legged, and leaned earnestly towards the priest.

"You see, you see what I mean? That impudent little snot even answers back the Padre? What incredible nerve!"

"An ignorant flea of a child –"

"Who's blasphemed the Holy Cross!"

"A miracle dragonfly then, if you wish – but a cross? Certainly not, Padre – enggggggg-chug-chug-chug-chug-enggggggg–" Pina leapt from the altar, landed amidst the open-mouthed crowd, walked through it, and out the church door, still with her airborne motions. "I tell you, it was a giant, beautiful flying thing – enggggg-chug-chug-chug-enggggg –"

Engggggggg – is that Pina's deep bass? *Halat nguna*, that's much louder and not human at all. Heavens, what's that? Everyone had followed Pina and her flight which seemed to be echoed somewhere – up there?

"Look, oh, look! The cross! The dragonfly! Ay, *Dios ko po!*" Inggo had forgotten his bad leg as he tried to stretch to his full height, waving both arms towards the sky.

"*Santa Maria, Ina nin Dios . . .*" Most of the crowd near-ly fell on each other as they crouched or knelt, then closed their eyes and bowed their heads, either in fear or in petri-fied adoration. One man kept on kissing the ground. Grandmother-in-the-knees began to say the rosary. Manay Elsa had visions of meeting the Pope. And Padre Biya sud-denly felt very sad and tired. The village had too much war indeed. Time for miracles now.

"No, no, don't kneel. Look up, look up!" Pina jumped up and down in frenzy. "You have to see it for what it is. See how its tail burns, and the eyes, ay – see the fire in them?"

The young pilot from Tennessee was back to reconnoitre the area for any more signs of the retreating Japanese, this time with renewed vigour and even elation after hearing how the US airforce had just mushroom-bombed Manila and thus thrashed the Japanese base. He felt like humming the American anthem as he adjusted his binoculars – but wait a minute, what's this? Hey, the natives are kneeling again! Gee, they sure love us around here. Damn, wish I had a camera!

He was most overcome, his chest began to swell, he felt. And his eyes stung a bit, when his vision picked up the little girl who was jumping up and down, arms reaching out to him – O, hail America! Must fly lower so these humble folk can see the flag on my tail, yes, take me closer to their level. Back in Manila, he loved it when the golden-brown girls came up to him and smiled, "Victory Joe!"

Yes, do a little dive, won't hurt really. Here we go – engggg-engggg – chug-chug-chug – gee, what a reception! – engggg-chug-chug-chug – lower, lower – chug-chug-ugh-ugh-ugh-ugh – what the – what's happening – what – Omigod!

"Ay, Pina, look – it's falling!" Inggo screamed.

"Ay! Ay! Ay! The heaven, the cross is falling!"

"Falling on our heads! We're all going to die! *Santa Maria* – !"

"*Madre de Dios*, it's coming towards – everyone, everyone get out of here! Run! Quickly! *Por Dios y por Santo*, run!" Padre Biya could hardly breathe as he drove his flock from the entrance of the church – to somewhere safe, over there, yes, under that *balete* tree! Everyone!

So this is how the world ends, Manay Elsa's last thought before she fainted into the arms of Grandmother-in-the-knees, just before the air grew dim and thundered, and the earth shook. Then all was still.

Not long after, Padre Biya opened his eyes. Clutching at his heart, knowing something he couldn't understand had broken there, he hurried to the sight of the crash, exactly at the doorstep of his church. Pina and Inggo followed close at his heels, the rest of the parishioners right behind them. Surprisingly, the cross-dragonfly was in one piece, though badly dented. And the man – there's a man in it! – was alive, ay, a miracle! Another one!

A man from heaven, imagine! And he's as white as the angels. Is he perhaps our *Anghel de la Guardia*? San Gabriel himself! Don't you come any closer, it's not proper. Hush, all of you. Only the Padre should – but Pina had already sped past the priest, dragging Inggo with her.

Squatting before the stunned pilot, she prodded him with a finger. "Yes, he's alive – but what is he?" She turned to the parish priest.

"You hurt, son?"

The crowd, who had now bravely crept forward, wondered at the Padre's strange tongue. Where did it come from?

"Here, take my hand." Padre Biya hadn't spoken English in a long time, the words tasted strangely in his mouth. "Can you stand – ?"

"Huh?" The angel from Tennessee was all right but very sore. It was hardly a pleasant trip from heaven.

"You must be really scared, falling a long way from the sky like that. No wonder you're so pale – but what are you – ?"

"Pina, Pina . . . ," Padre Biya pushed her gently aside. "It's okay, son. You're with good folk. Hoy, someone, come and help us here."

"So-o-o white . . . *Dios ko*, like our plaster saints . . ."

Someone swooned in devotion.

"So white . . . all blood must have left him, of course." Inggo was familiar with the symptom of fear.

"But – what are you?"

"Huh?" The poor pilot could not understand why a little girl was hovering around him in such an agitated manner and why there was no "Victory Joe" greeting from the crowd.

"What are you?" She tugged once more at his arm, but Padre Biya led him away.

Pina was terribly disappointed. She was wrong, utterly wrong in her story and, now, she couldn't think of another version to right it. She did not feel like following the procession of the faithful entering the church with the pale man, not at once. For a moment, she pondered over the possible answer to her important query before Inggo took her aside.

"Hoy, Pina," he whispered, "our dragonflies may not be as big or fancy as his, but – they surely fly better."

# DREAM STORIES

### 1. *Corazon*

The Spanish lady lived in a mansion which she tried to keep spotless. Sixteen rooms formed a square around a large atrium with a plain earth floor. No plants growing, as they disturbed the eye, and no spots of dirt if she had her way. Any floor must be well maintained; even soil must be clean.

She said her sister lived with her, but far away at the other side of the atrium, in the sixteenth room; she occupied the first. They were not on speaking terms. Her sister was frivolous and wasteful, and threw wild, dirty parties, so she decided to sell the house and move to a smaller place.

The day they were about to leave, her sister would not come out of her room. From the atrium, she called out to the sixteenth room, but no answer. It was nearly evening; she'd been calling out the whole day. The atrium was desolate and freezing, and all sixteen rooms were dark except for one lighted window. She knew she was in there. "Corazon,

Corazon!" she called. But no answer, just a silent light from the window.

In the morning, the new owner of the house found her crouched over her bags and very ill. Heart attack? He took her to hospital, but couldn't find anyone to inform about her condition. Records said, no relatives.

At the hospital, her heart X-ray perplexed the doctors. The organ was nowhere to be seen! "Because she wouldn't leave with me," the Spanish lady tried to explain, but they barely listened – "Corazon, Corazon, I called out to the sixteenth room, but she wouldn't even answer . . ."

## 2. Yellow

Her husband gave her a tiny box before he went on another long trip. In it was a fat, yellow chick not looking more than a day old. To amuse you while I'm away, he said. It was a new yellow, heaving quite abnormally. Its breathing filled the room. She couldn't stand the sound of yellow breathing within an enclosed space, so she left the room, the house. The breathing spread around the large lawn and disturbed even the flowers.

She had to do something. She replaced the lid on the box. But the breathing only intensified, as though the chick were dying loudly.

Loud death was bad luck, so she frantically searched for a way to dispose of it. But the breathing grew a voice. Save me, it said. Cut open my breast and take out my heart then plant it and save me. But she did not have a knife. She considered using her nails, but the thought of the messy act made her stomach turn. She ran around the lawn, holding the box with the dying yellow which was pleading to be divested of its heart.

When she reached the gate of her husband's estate, she couldn't stand the breathing or the pleading any longer. She flung the box away and fled to the house without looking back.

Her husband returned six months later. While inside her that night, he remarked about the pretty new shrubs at the gate. He congratulated her on the choice. Where did she get them, he asked, but in a knowing voice. They were just beginning to bloom, too, he said. Yellow flowers, chick yellow, no, a deeper shade actually. The yellow segments of ripe jackfruit hanging like succulent hearts.

### 3. The Death of Chopin Chopin

He made music, but went about the task carelessly, untidily. He left music everywhere, hung his notes wherever he found them. On his washcloth, the tap, the bedpost, even left them in the pantry among the cans of sardines, in his apron pocket, all over the floor. One day, he found a fat half-note embedded in his blueberry muffin. And the toilet got clogged with two quarter notes which refused to become unslurred.

The woman he lived with decided she'd had enough when a multitude of tiny sixteenth notes gathered like mould on her brand-new lingerie. After a final fight, while she was trying to extricate an eighth note out of her hair, she packed her bags and walked out. Never to come back.

He cared even less for tidying up. Music littered every corner of the house.

His landlord threatened to evict him, so he embarked on a general cleaning and swept all the music into his closet, which he locked afterwards. The notes were indignant and threatened to self-destruct if he did not let them out. But he kept the closet locked anyhow, until, one day, the music made good its threat. The closet exploded.

In the morning, he was found collapsed on the floor, clutching at his chest, crying about needles all over his heart. Doctor's diagnosis: severe angina. He died the following night.

When the landlord cleaned his flat for the next tenant, he discovered the mess. Strewn everywhere, the half notes, quarter notes, eighth and sixteenth notes were all looking fat and healthy, but missing their stems.

# SHOES

The little girl, about five, is hopping about and half-running behind the man with a large jute sack on his back. He is in his mid-twenties, but seems older. Occasionally, he puts his load down and squats beside her. She whispers something, he nods, and they're on their way again.

The asphalt road is burning. It smells and sticks to one's soles. She hops about in her new white shoes and blue poplin dress with a faded Donald Duck on the bodice. She is sweating heavily like him. She keeps hopping. Passers-by, who are going home to lunch, smile or frown to themselves. How can one play in this unbearable heat?

High noon and there are no trees. Just a long road under construction, lined with a motley of shops teetering between age and imposed newness, and looking quite startled by this state of affairs. A once sleepy town being rushed into progress.

The blue dress is soaked in sweat. Donald Duck looks

limp. Running to catch up, she nudges his leg with a finger. He stops and bends towards her. She whispers; he nods and lays down his sack. She sits on it and wipes her shoes with the hem of her dress. Meanwhile, he heads for a corner store a few metres away. He comes back with Coke in a plastic bag and two straws.

They sip it quietly in the middle of the half-constructed road.

She whispers to him again. This gesture of conspiratorially bending towards an ear somehow looks more intense than normal, as if the girl were telling him the major secrets of the world.

He takes off her shoes, bought especially for this outing. The soles of her feet are red, promising heat blisters. He examines the shoes, knocks at the soles. Thin plastic; inside, cardboard. He sighs and takes out a frayed rag from his pocket. He tears it in two then lays each half inside the shoes. They were a bargain from the street market.

She puts them back on and walks around the sack. Tight, but better now. She almost smiles. She has stopped hopping.

He proceeds to unpack the pouch tied to his side. Six boiled sweet potatoes, two pieces of dried fish and a coconut sweet for the girl. He spreads them on the sack beside the girl. They eat quietly.

The sweet is nibbled slowly, while she beats the sack with her heel in time with some silent rhythm. He makes a soft remark; she pops the last of the sweet into her mouth, then hurriedly stands up, brushing her dress. He rises, too, after packing and looks around, shading his eyes with a hand. Almost deserted now, the unfinished road seems endless.

He cocks his damp brow to the side, as if querying the still air, then shakes his head. He addresses her, she responds, softly again; expectedly, he nods. They walk towards the corner store to inquire –

"I CAN'T HEAR YOU –" The voice is too loud and gruff from behind several bales of hemp at the doorway.

"Please, may I ask –" His soft enquiry is drowned by a baby's wail from the adjacent house.

"TALK LOUDER, WILL YOU?"

"Please, where's –"

The baby screams with fervour.

"QUIET THERE!"

Its crying grows fainter, as if it were moved to the far end of the house.

"What do you want?" The voice emerges, a rotund septuagenarian munching a piece of pork fat. His short, sweaty singlet does not quite cover a beer-belly in progress.

That navel peeks rudely at me, the girl thinks and stares at her shoes instead. She squats behind a bale of hemp, trying to hide from the sun.

"I said, where is Mr Jose's house, please?"

The old man takes a while to speak. "Why?"

Silence, except for the continuous munching and a slight burp.

The man shifts his weight from one foot to the other. "We have business."

"What business?"

"We are – visiting."

"And just who are you?"

"Nestor. Nestor Capili, and I want to know where –"

The wrinkled face squints at the younger man. "Visiting, eh?"

The little girl shuffles her feet; the shoes are getting tighter, what with the rag padding. The old man notices her for the first time.

"And she's visiting, too?"

"Yes – we have something for him."

"Have you?" The old man moves to the half-opened door that leads to the adjacent house. He closes it before saying, "I'm Mr Jose."

"Oh–" The syllable is barely audible, just a breath dangling.

"And you have something – for me?" The old man seems to choose his words with care.

"Yes, sir, sweet potatoes here, a sackful, very good ones from your farm, sir." The gaunt face is trying to smile at the host, revealing bad teeth.

A slight hesitation. "Come in then."

Nestor drags the sack inside. The girl doesn't budge from the doorway. Her feet hurt.

"You come in, too."

She follows hesitantly, looking up for the first time. She makes out a cavern crowded with more bales of hemp, sacks of rice, an antiquated counter with a few jars of candy and biscuits, and a large, shining, obviously brand-new refrigerator, the only brightness in the store. The place is dark and musty. And too warm, it can curdle your thoughts.

She sits on the sack, which her father laid on the floor, and stares at her new shoes. They're not as white any more; the frill around the toes is limp and dusty. Ay, still pretty though tight.

"I know you don't know me, sir, because it's Manoy Nito who actually takes care of your farm, I'm his brother-in-law, by the way, and I've helped him with the planting and things since we moved to your land after the flood, and we're very grateful to you, of course, and I dug these sweet potatoes myself, you have good land, sir, very good, and I do help regularly, sir." The man's breath is running after each word. He keeps on wiping the sweat off his brow with the back of a grimy arm.

"You do?"

"Ay, yes sir, and I'll help again during the harvest . . . then I'll rebuild our old house once the water ebbs from the valley, then we won't have to impose on your kindness which we truly –"

"A farm on a hill is paradise, I say." The host rubs his belly contentedly, raising the short singlet even more. "So, you think I'll have a good harvest, eh?" The rude navel stares around the room like a moist eye.

"Of course, sir, it's very good land, very good . . . and safe." He wants to speed through the small talk and catch the right words for his real intention, even if Manoy Nito, his brother-in-law, warned him against saying it. He even strongly discouraged this visit.

"Nito's a good worker."

"Certainly, sir. And his sister, too, my wife –"

"You like a Coke, girl?" The old man leans against his shining fridge. "It's terribly warm in here, I know."

She shakes her head at the shoes. They seem to be getting smaller, pushing the toes and heels into a painful curl.

"My wife, sir – Trining – we're also visiting my –" There, he's said it.

The little girl looks up expectantly at the mention of her mother's name. For once, the indistinct face comes alive, acquiring a sudden personality, perhaps, even an incoming smile.

"I wonder – we're wondering – she still hasn't finished her job here?"

"She's not home at the moment."

The small face withdraws its engagement. Again, she crouches over her aching feet.

"Four months ago, she wrote – only once. Said she was coming home last month, sir." This fervid demeanour makes him look even more gaunt, bones pushing out, cheeks tight.

"The new maid hasn't arrived yet as promised, so Trining has to stay – a little longer, Nestor – Nestor, isn't it?"

"Yes . . ." His face sags. He runs a hand over it, less to wipe off the sweat than to stay this facial collapse, so characteristic of wretchedness.

"How about a biscuit, girl?"

She's not interested. She's trying to undo the buckle of a shoe.

"She hasn't seen her mother for almost a year now – can we wait till she comes back?" The plea is both lame and desperate.

Her little fingers cannot quite get the shoe off.

"She sends you her pay regularly, doesn't she?" The old man goes to the counter, takes out a candy from a jar, then offers it to the girl. "Here."

She does not even look up, her face bowed intently over the unruly shoe.

Mr Jose tut-tuts and pops the candy into his mouth. "Trining's on an errand in town. It will be a long day there for her."

"A long day . . . ?" Nestor surveys the seventy-four-year-old landlord of Manoy Nito, his brother-in-law.

After the flood, Nito offered his sister, Nestor's wife, as a housemaid for the master in exchange for her family's temporary shelter on his farm. And "temporary" became forever, because the floodwater would not ebb from the valley.

"She'll take a while yet, so you'll miss your boat if you wait."

The lie chokes him, as if it were shoved into his mouth. He feels tight around the throat. He can't tell him he knows, that he has always known so, softly, he echoes, "Yes, we will miss the boat."

His daughter stands up from the sack of sweet potatoes. She tugs at her father's pants. Again, the intense series of conspiratorial gestures – he stoops down, she whispers, he nods.

"What's her name?" The old man asks as he returns to rummaging behind the bales of hemp at the doorway. He has killed enough time with the visitors.

"Nining – well, tell her – tell her, please, to write, at least," Nestor can't quite uncurl the words in his throat.

"What did you say?" The landlord asks, without looking up from his task.

From the house, the baby wails as if in response.

Nestor listens, holding his breath, then lets go.

"You were saying – ?"

The small hand tugs more urgently.

"Nothing. Come, Nining."

But she wouldn't leave the doorway, so he bends down towards her, again with fervent care, as if he were receiving another major secret of the world. She whispers, he nods, then squats. He takes off her shoes, wraps them in the pouch at his side, and hoists her up on his shoulders, then strides off. The asphalt road is too hot to walk on, but they cannot miss the boat home.

# TRIPTYCH

### Watching

The crook of your
shoulder, a boat.
I am sinking into a
boat, I am rocking.
When you shrug
& my eye switches
to slow-mo, so your
left shoulder lifts
always higher than
the other in that soft
odd way – then I
think of sailing.

### Waiting

Sails promise to keep the
appointment at 3:00 in this
morning pillow, who cares?
Look, I billow half-hearted,
ventricle not quite unhinged
even as the water deepens
bluer than the sky still under
the lids. Nudge them, beg me
leap, unfurl as if life were
only about setting out to sea.
Willing to be Ahab's whale,
or else we drown in land.

### Waning

Wind on a diet. This
desire growing thin.
Breath settles on a scale
that registers zero &
I think me saved
from a tempest –
duress is beautiful.
Run aground the
flutter in the lungs.
About not feeding the
air to push a longing,
such is my conviction

as she longs & watches as he waits & longs as she wanes all longing to a
halt. At a boating party, Martha hopes Martin will turn around, return her

look, even vaguely, while he believes his wife, Mary, will hold him again, she who must stop wanting Martha. What soap opera, this doomed triad,

but a non-event, Sand & pebbles, I eat & quickly starve. No fasting really, I read in them but think wet could be sweeter & more your shrug as you between my legs, fumble profound. I am fashionably turn away, unaware of half-heartedness. Make thin, thighs so lean – flush of how I unfurl like me whole & full like a tingle ache in them even a mast. As clean as prow. Head of an eagle leaner now. No more the white of my eyes, almost alive again, potent launchings or moorings. O look. & come. statement against the sky. No wind, just that, no wind,

as we launch a trilogy. One hopes each story reads accurately on its own, even as these three plots of certainty sail into each other, reading so ambivalently. Martha, Martin, Mary. You can read them vertically or horizontally. Grounded on two feet – land is always steady after all. Or stretched like the earth itself, all the bumps & hollows more visible, body always uneven & vision blurred. & today, Martha, Martin, Mary are caught just like that. Supine. Stranded

on the edge, such A supplication: Mary, No trace of fat. Such
is the only way to be my captain astride redemption after all the
come. On a wish the prow. Before the bed nights of being wedged
on a shoulder, sinks – the twenty year between duty & desire,
I sail out, out to old golden band much gorgeously corpulent.
fuck the horizon. heavier now & gravity Now disarmed, deflated,
Martin, my name more keen. This eagle, made anorexic, Martha.
is Martha, listen. it cannot fly to save me. I am safe & O so light

for champagne – Mary celebrates on the upper deck. Her back to Martha & Martin.
At the wheel, he still imagines waking under Mary's fingers, while Martha tries to
catch his ungenerous eye. Everyone has gone. Boating party over & anchor down as

I stare, mast of my Weight of wait: whale That fades – the one
eyes white as wished- & eagle both, but only longed-for, as longing
for come. Whole orbs in a yearning so sharp, loses all wind & long-ers
gloriously coated cuts a hole on the bed. I fizzle out. All made
blind – & you vanish sink through & you don't thin, perspective pushed
just like that. Don't! even know, my love. to a vanishing point.

# BORDER LOVER

Wore it on a tree
after my long flight

Right after my long flight,
I wore it on a tree,
under the banana leaves

Right after my long flight,
I wore it on a tree,
under a canopy of green flags,
my banana heart,
magenta velveteen and just
beginning to open . . .

There, Grandmother, this should make you happy. I'm now
breathing Western air, flying back to my "White Land", as
you call it, yet I'm still your tropical baby, trust me. What
with all these doodles about the banana flowers just outside
your window –

"*Puso ki batag*, banana heart. I'll cook you one in coconut
milk with enough chilli to make you cry. Wasn't that your
favourite dish, ha?"

What a welcome, you brandishing the wooden ladle under my nose! And still inquiring whether they ever feed me rice, cooked properly, back there in my Australia.

"Ay, *siyempre*, Gran, of course, Oz is – multicultural!"

"Inday, Inday, come home, please / Even if you kill me / I'll never do it again" – ah, you had to sing that ditty again, something about infidelity – but, Granny-O, I do come home every year to visit you, don't I? But you'd grown funny this time. You said you stared hard at my plane's bum, wondering whether it would ever touch ground.

I, too, wondered about how it is to really land. Three weeks ago, as the plane descended on our province, I marvelled at the different shades of green – deep on the fronds of coconuts, shimmering on banana leaves, cool on the stretch of grass and monochrome on the various shrubs I could not even name – now, with the Sydney vegetation rushing up to greet me as I touch down, same thing . . . eucalypt, eucalypt, and . . . eucalypt . . . ? Yes, I don't know how it is to land and not land, my wings rearranging themselves for home and not home.

"*Daeng problema*. If you lose your way home, because of the tricks of the spirits, just turn your dress inside out."

"And I'm supposed to find my way, really?"

Okay, I'll try it sometime, Gran. Turn my heart inside out, like a wallet, and shake out all its failed currency, its futile medium of exchange. Peso, dollar, peso, dollar, peso . . . she loves me, she loves me not, she loves me, she loves me not – she who keeps her money close to her heart, wrapped in an old handkerchief that smells of Tiger Balm, all that "loose change" for the rainy days pinned under her blouse, with her *puso ki batag*, ay, her banana heart. It shoots forth a red, oh, no, a magenta velveteen –

Flirting, three layers of heartskin
flying in the air

My petticoated flirt:
three layers of heartskin unfurled
in the air,
à la Monroe flashing
not pale legs,
but tiny yellow fingers
strung into a filigree of topazes.

"Hoy, *anong gusto mo* – what would you like it cooked with
– dried fish or shrimp paste?" Grandmother had just prepared the heart for the wok.

"Oh, I don't know. Up to you, Gran."

Me of the banana heart with its tell-tale fingers drum-
ming at the seams – I was getting pretty restless in her
kitchen then and suddenly inspired into a serious chat with
the wall – yeah, yeah, I've got a banana heart for my head
and, each time I unfurl, I wear a different face speaking a
strange tongue. My dialect Bikol, then Filipino, then
English, all mixed up, broken into an almost infantile blab-
ber – akin to Kristeva's semiotic? Ah, these little epiphanies.
Not bad after three years of postgrad meanderings in
Australia.

"What are you muttering there, hoy?"

The "semiotic" as opposed to the "symbolic" which
defines identity – a rationalised self-representation? Well,
who am I anyway – ?

"*Aysus*, buzzing to the wall again, like a mosquito – who
are you? Of course you're my granddaughter, who, after flying to your Australia to write – what's it again – a *tisis*?
Sounds like an affliction of the lungs to me, *tisis*!"

"Thesis, Grandmother."

"Whatever – and now she comes home with a strange
tongue which she practises on her poor Grandmother.

*Ano ka*, you turning up your nose on me?"

Six-thirty p.m., past the Angelus, and Gran was sulking. In the tropical dusk outside, her banana orchard came alive with hearts minted into red-gold, fake-gold petticoats unfolding, the rest of them still closed. Ay, the smell of dry leaves burning, the murmur of dialect, the occasional chirping of the first nightbird, the comfort of tropical domesticity . . . and the time it took to prepare a meal there – from scratch!

I walked to my poor, stooped Grandmother slaving before the stove and hugged her from behind, playfully lifting her thin frame – she was oh-so-sweet with coconut milk, fish sauce and lemon grass.

"Hoy, *pagparakaraw-karaw baya* – put me down! Put me down!"

I told her it was not a put-down when I spoke to her about what I learned from the West. Look at me, Gran, I made it – there in White Land. Western thought has allowed me entry into their arts, their academies.

"Their thought? What about your thought, our thought back here? *Aber daw*, are they interested in what I have to say as well, ha?"

"That's beside the point, Grandmother. Look, Western thought can be so – so empowering. How to explain – yes, for instance, feminism had saved me –"

"*Ano*? Pimini – piminisim? Just what are you saying, you silly –"

"Oh, yes, Gran, here's a perfect example. Feminism had saved me from the enslavement of the kitchen and had opened inspiring and once unimaginable doors for me – and it could have saved you, too, you know, from all this toiling before your bloody old stove, if only –"

"*Anong pakiaram ninda* – I love my stove. LEAVE MY

STOVE ALONE!"

Tough customer, of course, my Grandma who seemed to cook forever. I never broached the subject again, my "silly piminism", she called it, not after she said I had gouged out her heart with strange talk. Yes, of course, none of that stuff and, if she were here, certainly none of these fancy squiggles on paper, this in-flight poetic gush about her banana heart – why not put it in the wok instead, child?

> Yesterday, Grandmother plucked it,
> desecrating aesthetics and romance,
> this sacrilegious twist

> But yesterday,
> Grandmother plucked it,
> stripped it to the core,
> desecrating aesthetics and romance,
> and cut it in two –

See, Gran, here's the proof of my loyalty. I'm due to land in Sydney, but I'm still writing about your banana heart and your irrepressible kitchen discourse, naturally –

> One half she served fresh,
> dressed in vinegar;
> the other, she cooked in coconut milk and chilli
> while humming about young girls
> who fly to learn strange ideas
> in a stranger tongue.

"Necessity, Grandmother. Where I'm at, I need to speak this tongue, but the mouth is still your granddaughter's, of course – *bilinga baya* – yes, just take a look –"

"Ay, my clever, foolish one," she said, pulling my chin in that familiar affectionate gesture. "You are no longer you, and you know that – here –" she knocked at her heart then went about preparing the coconut. She would not look at me.

"Hey, Gran, give me that. I'll grate it." I could smell a sulk a mile away.

"What would you know – ?"

She had stuck to the old ways. For years, I had advised her to get an electric coconut grater, but, no – it still had to be a tedious job on what we call a "horse", a makeshift, low and very narrow rectangular seat with a fringed steel blade at one end.

"Haven't done this for a long time, but I'm still quite good at it – see?"

Of course, a knowledge in the bones, like the taste and smell of home cooking, as sharply etched in the memory as dried fish frying. The whole house smogs over with the delicious stench and you know you're home again, in the bones.

"Hoy, make it fine, *baya*. No, not that way . . . too big, those shreds . . . *ano nang* . . . ," she scolded.

"I know, I know. *Nasa buto*, Grandma. Grating a coconut is a knowledge in the bones – trust me."

But something strange stirred in them, the marrow was changing colour. I heard it, saw it, smelled it. My English she considered un-Filipino and my "accented dialect", she found even more strange – "*siguro*, you now have a new heartbeat as well, and we're all out of step here" – then, in her banana orchard, the memory of the white light of Australian winter, pale as a naked pear, and all the shades of Oz crept in. And the fragrance of fish and chips with vinegar impinged on the sharp sourness of her fish soup, rose-coloured with young, sweet potato leaves –

"Hoy, what are you daydreaming about, ha? You want to grate your hand, too, you silly girl?" She called out while shredding the banana heart. "Quickly now with that grating or we'll be eating at midnight – ay, too slow, too slow –"

> Later, plying me with more rice,
> she said, "Here. Two dishes
> from one heart."

It was a quiet last meal together. But I've grown accustomed to this. Every time I arrive for my yearly visit, she's all chatter, then, at the end of my stay, she cooks all my favourite dishes, fusses and scolds. And during the meal, which begins with her urging me to eat more, eat more, you skinny girl, her speech is reduced to monosyllables. Then she clams up. The next day, she always refuses to take me to the airport –

> Later, plying me with more rice,
> in the dialect, she said,
> "Honi. Duwang putahe hale sa sarong puso."
> "Here. Two dishes from one heart."
> I could not eat,
> not on a hollow growing,
> peculiar in my breast.

> Flight PR 278, Sydney Airport,
> 10 June 1996

A poem at touchdown, how about that, Granny-O? Yes, I have gouged out your heart all right, your banana heart now duly transformed into fancy squiggles on paper. Of course, everything is a bloody grist for the mill, really, everything – trust me.

# THE SADNESS COLLECTOR

And she will not stop eating, another pot, another plate, another mouthful of sadness, and she will grow bigger and bigger, and she will burst.

On the bed, six-year-old Rica braces herself, waiting for the dreaded explosion –

Nothing. No big bang. Because she's been a good girl. Her tears are not even a mouthful tonight. And maybe their neighbours in the run-down apartment have been careful, too. From every pot and plate, they must have scraped off their leftover sighs and hidden them somewhere unreachable. So Big Lady can't get to them. So she can be saved from bursting.

Every night, no big bang really, but Rica listens anyway.

The house is quiet again. She breathes easier, lifting the sheets slowly from her face – a brow just unfurrowing, but eyes still wary and a mouth forming the old, silent question – are you really there? She turns on the lamp. It's girlie kitsch like the rest of the decor, from the dancing lady wallpaper to the row of Barbie dolls on a roseate plastic table. The tiny room is all pink bravado, hoping to compensate for the warped ceiling and stained floor. Even the unhinged window flaunts a family of pink paper rabbits.

Are you there?

Her father says she never shows herself to anyone. Big Lady only comes when you're asleep to eat your sadness. She goes from house to house and eats the sadness of everyone, so she gets too fat. But there's a lot of sadness in many houses, it just keeps on growing each day, so she can't stop eating, and can't stop growing, too.

Are you really that big? How do you wear your hair?

*Dios ko*, if she eats all our mess, Rica, she might grow too fat and burst, so be a good girl and save her by not being sad – hoy, stop whimpering, I said, and go to bed. Her father is not always patient with his storytelling.

All quiet and still now. She's gone.

Since Rica was three, when her father told her about Big Lady just after her mother left for Paris, she has always listened intently to all the night-noises from the kitchen. No, that sound is not the scurrying of mice – she's actually checking the plates now, lifting the lid off the rice pot, peeking into cups for sadness, both overt and unspoken. To Rica, it always tastes salty, like tears, even her father's funny look each time she asks him to read her again the letters from Paris.

She has three boxes of them, one for each year, though the third box is not even half-full. All of them tied with Paris ribbons. The first year, her mother sent all colours of the rainbow for her long, unruly hair, maybe because her father did not know how to make it more graceful. He must have written her long letters, asking about how to pull the mass of curls away from the face and tie them neatly the way he gathered, into some semblance of order, his own nightly longings.

It took some time for him to perfect the art of making a pony-tail. Then he discovered a trick unknown to even the best hairdressers. Instead of twisting the bunch of hair to make sure it does not come undone before it's tied, one can rotate the whole body. Rica simply had to turn around in place, while her father held the gathered hair above her head. Just like dancing, really.

She never forgets, *talaga naman*, the aunties whisper among themselves these days. A remarkable child. She was only a little thing then, but she noticed all, didn't she, never missed anything, committed even details to memory. A very smart kid, but too serious, a sad kid.

They must have guessed that, recently, she has cheated on her promise to behave and save Big Lady. But only on nights when her father comes home late and drunk, and refuses to read the old letters from Paris – indeed, she has been a very good girl. She's six and grown up now, so, even if his refusal has multiplied beyond her ten fingers, she always makes sure that her nightly tears remained small and few. Like tonight, when she hoped her father would come home early, as he promised again. Earlier, Rica watched TV to forget, to make sure the tears won't amount to a mouthful. She hates waiting. Big Lady hates that, too, because then she'll have to clean up till the early hours of the morning.

Why Paris? Why three years – and even more? *Aba*, this is getting too much now. The aunties can never agree with her mother's decision to work there, on a fake visa, as a domestic helper – ay, *naku*, taking care of other people's children, while, across the ocean, her own baby cries herself to sleep? *Talaga naman!* She wants to earn good money and build us a house. Remember, I only work in a factory . . . Her father had always defended his wife, until recently, when all talk about her return was shelved. It seems she must extend her stay, because her employer might help her to become "legal". Then she can come home for a visit and go back there to work some more –

The lid clatters off the pot. Beneath her room, the kitchen is stirring again. Rica sits up on the bed – the big one has returned? But she made sure the pot and plates were clean, even the cups, before she went to bed. She turns off the lamp to listen in the dark. Expectant ears, hungry for the phone's overseas beep. Her mother used to call each month and write her postcards, also long love letters, even if she couldn't read yet. With happy snaps, of course. Earlier this year, she sent one of herself and the new baby of her employer.

Cutlery noise. Does she also check them? This has never happened before, her coming back after a lean meal. Perhaps, she's licking a spoon for any trace of saltiness, searching between the prongs of a fork. Unknown to Rica, Big Lady is wise, an old hand in this business. She senses that there's more to a mouthful of sadness than meets the tongue. A whisper of salt, even the smallest nudge to the palate, can betray a century of hidden grief. Perhaps, she understands that, for all its practice, humanity can never conceal the daily act of futility at the dinner table. As we feed continually, we also acknowledge the perennial nature of our hunger. Each time we bring food to our mouths, the gut-emptiness that we attempt to fill inevitably contaminates our cutlery, plates, cups, glasses, our whole table. It is this residual contamination, our individual portions of grief, that she eats, so we do not die from them – but what if we don't eat? Then we can claim self-sufficiency, a fullness from birth, perhaps. Then we won't betray our hunger.

But Rica was not philosophical at four years old, when she

had to be cajoled, tricked, ordered, then scolded severely before she finished her meal, if she touched it at all. Rica understood her occasional hunger strikes quite simply. She knew that these dinner quarrels with her father, and sometimes her aunties, ensured dire consequences. Each following day, she always made stick drawings of Big Lady with an ever-increasing girth, as she was sure the lady had had a big meal the night before.

Mouth curved downward, she's sad like her meals. No, she wears a smile, she's happy because she's always full. Sharp eyes, they can see in the dark, light-bulb eyes, and big teeth for chewing forever. She can hardly walk, because her belly's so heavy, she's pregnant with leftovers. No, she doesn't walk, she flies like a giant cloud and she's not heavy at all, she only looks heavy. And she doesn't want us to be sad, so she eats all our tears and sighs. But she can't starve, can she? Of course, she likes sadness, it's food.

Fascination, fear and a kinship drawn from trying to save each other. Big Lady saves Rica from sadness; Rica saves Big Lady from bursting by not being sad. An ambivalent relationship, confusing, but certainly a source of comfort. And always Big Lady as object of attention. Those days when Rica drew stick-drawings of her, she made sure the big one was always adorned with pretty baubles and make-up. She even drew her with a Paris ribbon to tighten her belly. Then she added a chic hat to complete the picture.

Crimson velvet with a black satin bow. Quite a change from all the girlie kitsch – that her mother had dredged from Paris' unfashionable side of town? The day it arrived in the mail, Rica was about to turn six. A perfect Parisienne winter hat for a tiny head in the tropics. It came with a bank-draft for her party.

She did not try it on, it looked strange, so different from

the Barbies and pink paper rabbits. This latest gift was unlike her mother, something was missing. Rica turned it inside out, searching – on TV, Magic Man can easily pull a rabbit or a dove out of his hat, just like that, always. But this tale was not part of her father's repertoire. He told her not to be silly when she asked him to be Magic Man and pull out Paris – but can she eat as far as Paris? Can she fly from here to there overnight? Are their rice pots also full of sad leftovers? How salty?

Nowadays, her father makes sure he comes home late each night, so he won't have to answer the questions, especially about the baby in the photograph. So he need not improvise further on his three-year-old tall tale.

There it is again, the cutlery clunking against a plate – or scraping the bottom of a cup? She's searching for the hidden mouthfuls and platefuls and potfuls. Cupboards are opened. No, nothing there, big one, nothing – Rica's eyes are glued shut. The sheets rise and fall with her breathing. She wants to leave the bed, sneak into the kitchen and check out this most unusual return and thoroughness.

That's the rice pot being overturned –

Her breaths make and unmake a hillock on the sheets –

A plate shatters on the floor –

Back to a foetal curl, knees almost brushing chin –

Another plate crashes –

She screams –

The pot is hurled against the wall –

She keeps screaming as she runs out of the room, down to the kitchen –

And the cutlery, glasses, cups, more plates –

Big Lady's angry, Big Lady's hungry, Big Lady's turning the house upside down –

Breaking it everywhere –

Her throat is weaving sound, as if it were all that it ever knew –

"SHUT UP – !"

Big Lady wants to break all to get to the heart of the matter, where it's saltiest. In the vein of a plate, within the aluminium bottom of a pot, in the copper fold of a spoon, deep in the curve of a cup's handle –

Ropes and ropes of scream –

"I SAID, SHUT UP!"

Her cheek stings. She collapses on the floor before his feet.

"I didn't mean to, *Dios ko po*, I never meant to –"

Her dazed eyes make out the broken plates, the dented pot, the shards of cups, glasses, the cutlery everywhere –

He's hiccupping drunkenly all over her –

"I didn't mean to, Rica, I love you, baby, I'll never let you go –" His voice is hoarse with anger and remorse.

"She came back, Papa –"

"She can't take you away from me –"

"She's here again –"

"Just because she's 'legal' now –"

"She might burst, Papa –"

"That whore – !" His hands curl into fists on her back.

Big Lady knows, has always known. This feast will last her a lifetime, if she does not burst tonight.

# BEFORE THE MOON RISES

Because I am deaf, they think I cannot hear. These men in green bark words past, above, around, but never towards me. It is all very sad, the blankness of their eyes, the tightness of their lips and their knuckles as white as eye-balls. Move, move, they urge everyone with the butt of their guns. I sit on my bamboo stairs and watch them oversee the villagers filing past with their meagre possessions. Everyone is leaving home while the chickens roost, because the government does not believe in chickens roosting. Not even in lighting the evening fire to boil the rice. Nor in gathering for the evening meal. It only believes in catching rebels. The soldiers said so when they ordered the whole village to evacuate. Away, away, the guns waved towards the forest. Quick, before the moon rises. And no one must come back.

As I am supposed to be deaf, I light my fire instead. Any moment now, the rice would boil. I had even set aside some dried fish to fry and a few wild tomatoes. A stray dog whines, scratching its behind against my stairs. It knows this is the only hut preparing supper. It shares my belief – the chickens have roosted, so we must get on with the end of the day. But no one notices our conspiracy. Everyone is anxious to beat the rising of the moon. Before the moon rises, the soldiers bark. The dog whines again. I throw it a dried fish. Perhaps, between the two of us, the moon will not rise tonight.

A baby's cry is smothered on its mother's breast. A few men whisper angrily among themselves. An old woman is weeping softly into her skirt. Because it is hushed, this leave-taking is too loud for me. No one knows this though. In this new hut of *kogon* grass and bamboo, I am apart from all their restrained frenzy, because everyone has forgotten me.

When I first arrived, the villagers had regarded me with much apprehension. I must have struck them as a strange vision. A very old woman, shrivelled and dark as a coconut husk, trailing long white hair to her ankles as she carried trunks of bamboo from the forest. How can she be so strong? The mothers and fathers were convinced I was evil, so they asked their children to keep away from "that stranger". Thus, from a distance, they watched me build this hut. At first, they suspiciously eyed my sharp tabak clearing the *kogon* grass; after some time, they grew braver. They began to mimic my posture.

She is so bent, she's almost kissing the ground. She wants to kiss carabao dung! She wants to kiss carabao dung! They followed me around for two weeks, but got tired, because I was so quiet. They told their parents I was harmless and probably deaf, because I did not mind their taunting. *Buktot na, bungog pa* – not only bent, but deaf as well.

This dog's masticating is a sad sound. It does not stop even after the dried fish is gone. I have forgotten how many times I've heard this sound before. Hunger is undeniably animal and it does not shut up. Ay, the sound of mastication will soon rise with the moon, with many moons, into a crescendo of a hungry village choir in the forest. Before the moon rises – bah! These soldiers will return to their camps and meat and rice and beer! The village? Probably in the forest, probably surviving. Just another evacuated village after all. Can't help it. The rebels must be hunted. Cut all avenues of aid or escape.

"Bantay! There's Bantay, Mamay!"

A young girl is running towards my hut followed by a woman dragging a heavy bag. As if they were coming home so soon. The dog wags its tail.

"She took my dog." She points a grubby finger at me and sucks it, in between bouts of accusation.

"Nene, we have no time for dogs." The mother's voice is tight. She does not look at me.

"*Bungog* is not leaving like us? Hey, listen everyone, 'the deaf one' is not leaving like us!" The girl shrieks at a few villagers who have followed her to my hut. Her eyes are bulging.

"I say, the deaf one does not want to leave with us!"

The mother yanks the girl from my stairs and hits her loudly on the bottom. She howls. The mother drops the bag and kneels weeping before the dog. It licks her hand.

"Really? How could she stay?"

"Doesn't she know?"

"She's deaf, can't you see?"

A group of meddlers begin to gather before my hut. I should not want to invite them to rice and dried fish and tomatoes before the moon rises.

"Do the soldiers know?"

"Aren't you going, too?"

A hysterical giggle. "Don't ask. Can't you see she's as deaf as a bat?"

"What's all this racket?"

A soldier has arrived. He parts the crowd with his gun. The youngest of them, I suppose, only a boy really. He steps back when he sees me. He stares at my long white hair which the dog is trying to catch with its paw. The crowd falls silent. The boy hesitates for a while then barks at me to get going, a rather feeble bark. He clutches the heavy gun too tightly, as if it would run away. The crowd titters.

"She's deaf, stone-deaf. You have to explain with your face, with actions."

Power positions shift. The boy looks at me then at the slightly jeering crowd.

"Go on, go on. Tell the deaf one to leave her house, too. See if you can make her."

The boy hesitates, then begins to wave his gun towards me and the forest. His green body hops about. I think of a praying mantis giving directions. He is making me sadder every minute.

"The rice is boiling. I have to attend to it, or else it will burn." I leave the confused boy and the laughing crowd.

"*Putang ina mo* – your mother's a whore!" He swears after me. I hear his steps on my bamboo stairs.

"Ay, your mother should burn your tongue, talking to your elder like that," someone from the crowd tut-tuts.

The steps halt.

"Yes, burn your tongue with chilli, I say."

"Go back to your mother, boy, and make her teach you some manners!"

"Not only the hottest chilli, but the stick, that's what you need."

"*Putang ina, n'yo* – all your mothers are whores!"

"*Hala*, your tongue might break out in rashes if you –"

A shot rings just as I lift the lid off the pot. I rush back to my doorstep. All the soldiers are rushing to my doorstep. The whole village seems to be rushing to my doorstep. All before the moon rises.

"I didn't mean to – I didn't mean to." The boy is shaking before the young girl who is bleeding profusely.

"*Bungog* is a jinx!"

"The deaf one is bad luck!"

"She's evil! Didn't I tell you? Maybe, she's really a witch!"

"She must not come with us!"

"Look out. She wants to touch her. Don't let her. No, don't –"

The girl is alive, but with a severe thigh wound. I examine it gingerly. The crowd takes in a breath in unison, as if I had betrayed each of their wounds. They do not stop me. They are afraid. I rip the hem of my skirt and proceed to make a tourniquet.

"You have blood under your eye, boy," I turn to the shaking lad kneeling before his victim. He begins to weep as if his heart would break.

The soldiers, who were momentarily stunned by our little drama, are jolted by the boy's hysteria. The tallest of them, obviously the leader, slaps "the sissy" then barks at the crowd to get going. Everyone begins to bark all at once. No time for this, no time. The boy is crying uncontrollably now. He seems to be more grief-stricken than the girl's mother. "Take her into my hut," I tell him.

"We have no time for this, old woman," the leader says.

"We will make time."

"And who are you to – ?"

"I am Selma of the North and South, and, I say, we will make time."

The village is hushed. Not because of my temerity, but because this is the first time they hear my name.

"Insolent hag!" The soldier points his gun at me. I hear the tightening of everyone's gut in the crowd. I start binding the girl's thigh. He kneels, aiming the gun at my temple. I watch his trigger finger whiten, whiter than his eyeballs. The sobbing boy screams. I pluck a strand of my hair and tie it around the prodding muzzle, push it aside, then begin to chant.

> "*Hare baya, Nonoy,*"
> *sabi kang bulan.*
> "*Hare baya, Nonoy,*
> *pagkawati ang saldang.*"

The soldier fidgets. He stares at the muzzle and then at my white hair trailing before his feet. His eyes glaze over. He drops his gun. The breathing of the village ebbs and flows like the tide.

> "Don't, my Son,"
> the moon said.
> "Don't, my Son,
> play with the sun."

He drops to his knees, pawing my hair like a dog. I rub the young girl's blood on the back of his hand. He whines and offers his palm to be rubbed as well. Some of the villagers search the sky for the moon.

> "*Hare baya, Nonoy,*"
> *sabi kang bulan.*
> "*Hare baya, Nonoy,*
> *paghaluna ang saldang.*"

He lifts the young girl. I follow them to my hut.

> "Don't my Son,"
> said the moon.
> "Don't, my Son,
> swallow the sun."

The whole village follows them to my hut – ay, I have done it again. Selma, the storyteller of the North and South, has done it again. Didn't I promise myself that, on my hundredth year, I would wait for my last days peacefully in a hut apart from people and their stories? I promised not to care any more. I had seen and heard too many stories by now and had told them many times over. But the young girl had to come looking for her dog. She had to set me to my old task again.

Now I have the village in my hut. Another people must be told stories, so they can hear the forgotten tale in each drop of blood that they spill. Every tale which dries up and dies when it leaves the body. What nuisance! On my hundredth year, I will be asked to sing their blood again, so they can understand and change their history. So they can keep the moon from rising.

"*Nanay* Selma, tell us a story." *Mother* Selma? The tallest green man had curled at my feet beside the dog. Neither barks.

"Tell us a story about wounds." The young girl's mother, now quite calm, stems the flow of blood, while I probe for the bullet.

"A story about tears." The weeping boy has cupped his tears and drunk them. He must be very thirsty after a long day of barking.

"About going away."

"About the forest."

"About the moon before it rises."

The whole village make demands while exploring my hut. With each step they take, the hut expands, as if trying to accommodate all. This ridiculous generosity is slipping from my fingers, pushing the *kogon* walls to expand. My hut has become the village. Look, they have overtaken me again, fingering my beads of the rainbow on the wall, hovering over some bones near the fire.

"Pearl grey," a voice behind me intones.

"Are they human ones?"

"Don't touch them."

"Your fingers might rot. You never know . . ."

The hushed voices are drowned by several babies bawling in synchronised hunger. The mothers bare their breasts. A young man farts too loudly. The children giggle and tease. Some of the soldiers suggest that the grief-stricken boy lie down to keep his tears from spilling. A grandfather says it's a good idea. Everyone talks all at once, trying to give advice. The hut trembles with all their home-noises holding back the rising of the moon.

"Ay, *lintian* – may the lightning strike you!" The young girl curses me in her pain. Her mother shushes her. The whole village and the soldiers echo the chiding sound while embarrassedly searching my face.

The bullet is a little devil on my palm. I return it to the weeping boy and begin to chew some herbs for the wound. It occurs to me that I had burnt the rice and that there is not enough dried fish and tomatoes for everyone.

# FROCK

Silvery fish on each breast. A trail of green turtles around the waist. He blinks and looks again as Aunt Emilia turns towards the door. A fin quivers.

"Hello . . ." she says with a mournful lilt in the "o".

A cold draught tails the big man. She shivers. A fish grows fat with a nipple.

"Emmy, Emmy . . ." he kind of croons in a big man's way.

She hesitates at first before shutting the door behind him. A flipper makes a tiny backstroke, just above her tummy. Secretly, of course.

From under the table, Bobby stares at these goings-on. He's nearly nine and extremely curious.

An arm circles her waist. The turtles are hidden and the fishes press close to his chest. Watch it, mister, oh, you'll hurt them, you'll squeeze them dead!

Bobby can hardly breathe, imagining the damage to the little swimmers on her dress, her sea-dress, he calls it. An iridescent blue, green, and even pink sometimes? Bobby thinks it's trying to confuse him, playing tricks under the sun or lamp, and even the glare from TV just now. But while he can't decide on the exact hue, he's quite certain that the little prints come to life occasionally and glow. Two fishes and eight turtles. He counted the latter several times, right after she arrived, just to make sure.

"Come home . . ." The big man's arm makes it ripple.

Bobby fidgets. He's trying to get a better look at how the arm does it, make the cloth move like that.

His favourite frock, but Aunt Emilia doesn't know this, of course. He hasn't told her, well, can't really, because his most beautiful Aunt always locks herself up in her room or in the bath – she takes very long baths. For the fishes and turtles, of course, Bobby reckons. He imagines she steps into the bath fully clothed, so the creatures can have a dip with her in water that always smells of lavender.

"No, Rodney, please . . ."

Bobby likes to eavesdrop on this event. He hears a wee splash every now and then. A fish diving from her breast, no, a turtle taking off from her waist, surely. Leaning against the bathroom door, he memorises the sound-shifts of her body, a leg curling up to give the turtles more room, perhaps, an arm stretched like driftwood for a fish to blow bubbles to.

"It will be okay now, after . . ."

Then he bathes after her, so he can check that no fish or turtle has gone down the drain. She tries not to look at him when she comes out, all moist and sniffly, always sniffly and red in the eyes as though she were catching a cold. He wants to ask about the creatures, but his mother warns him not to bother poor Auntie, because she isn't well so we have to be very nice to her for the few days when she's here and so on and so on. His mother always has a string of worries.

"I didn't go."

"You didn't . . . ?"

"No." Her voice is low and flat.

He holds her too tightly. "But Emmy . . ."

"YOU MUSN'T CRUSH THEM, MISTER – !"

She jumps out of the embrace – "Bobby again, Bobby everywhere."

The boy crawls out of his secret den.

"Eavesdropping will burn your ears, if you don't take care." She walks towards the culprit.

Her skirt is so close, blue this time, underwater blue. The hem nearly brushes his face as he stands. He is a tiny boy with a perpetually quizzical expression.

"Hello, Bobby," the man says.

He ignores the proffered big hand. "They'll die if you don't take care, with him."

Silence. She stares at the boy, looking perplexed for a moment, then forgets him. "Die, die . . . ," she mumbles to the wall. "Whatever can die, Rodney?"

"Emmy . . ."

"Your two fishes and eight turtles, of course." Bobby is in earnest.

She can't stop giggling, the fishes and turtles are shaking, they all think he's being funny, except the man. The frock moves away, it's blue but turning green as you stare at it longer, like now, with flashes of pink if you close then suddenly open your eyes. On her hips, sometimes on her back, or on her tummy. It never stays in one place, no, never, this pink.

"You said you'd do it . . ." Suddenly, the man looks very unhappy.

Aunt Emilia keeps studying the wall, hugging her arms around the two fishes, as if they were cold.

The turtles are hidden by the table. Bobby is almost tempted to peek under it to see what they're up to this time. He fiddles with the lace tablecloth, raring to lift it and then go under. He is oblivious to their conversation; it's a little slow and strained. His mother is working hard to make it gallop along, but with little success.

"Emilia should stay with us for a while, until you two can sort it out before – before the wedding? Have you chosen a church? I suggest you –"

"Sister, oh dear sister Edna, we can't sort it out, because I didn't go, did I?" Aunt Emilia's giggles are multiplying with each glass of wine. "Did I, Rodney?" Her black curls look strange, like a dark halo gone wild.

"Go?" Edna turns to Rodney who turns away. He doesn't know where to put his big arms.

The fishes echo her giggles. Was that a flick of the fin or the tail? And where they swim, the water is incandescent, blue-green-pink with candlelight flickers. Bobby is hopelessly enamoured. The creatures have never looked so alive.

She catches him staring. "My strange nephew likes my fish." She passes a thumb over her breast, making a little circle around a blue tail.

Bobby feels warm all over, he doesn't know why.

"You're drunk, Emilia," his mother sighs, checking her nape for hair which might have strayed from a perfect chignon. She always does this when she's worried.

"But Rodney likes my fish even better, don't you, Rodney – but only the fish."

"I don't know what's your problem, Emmy, you never tell me anything, really, you arrived here in a huff, on another rare, emotional visit, and I took you in and didn't ask questions, but you wouldn't ... you said you got engaged ..." She sounds impatient, she can't find any stray hair.

"My fishes got very much engaged." She cups her breasts. The fins sway slightly and the water ripples. "You love them so much, don't you, Rodney?" She winks at Bobby.

"Hush, Emilia!" His mother taps her chignon, as though censuring it.

"Fishes, yes, but other little creatures, no. Not when they get in the way to happiness – well, here's to happiness then." She drains her glass. Her neck is so white against the blue.

"Sorry, Edna, she shouldn't have bothered you . . ."

"My sister hasn't changed at all, Rodney."

"Not a bit. I love an audience, don't I?"

"Let's just go home, Emmy. We'll drive back tonight."

"And we'll be oh-okay?"

"Yes, of course, sweetie . . ." He puts an arm around her.

Bobby sits up, anticipating another lethal hug.

"You don't like Uncle Rodney, do you, kid?" Aunt Emilia leans towards him. The fishes seem to blink, eager for a reply.

"Stop teasing, Emmy." Edna sighs again. She has been given to sighing ever since her sister arrived. "We'll leave you two alone . . ."

"To sort it out." Aunt Emilia's giggle gets caught in her throat.

When Bobby creeps back to the dining room and under the table, all is hushed, the edgy atmosphere now softened and a bit warm, no, moist. He's damp around the collar and he is frantic. He cannot see the turtles. They seem to have run away. A big hand slides up and down the frock. In the darkness, it's almost black, a muddied blue-green. The hand disappears under it, perhaps searching for the turtles like him.

Aunt Emilia is breathing strangely, as if she were dying.

She's not having her nightly bath. She's just locked in her room. He's in there, too. Bobby hears them, her soft weeping, his sighing, then their sighing.

Bobby can't sleep. He imagines that, in the next room, a big hand is catching a fish by the tail or crushing a turtle's shell. And all the creatures are trying to swim out of the frock, because the big hand is all over it. But there's nowhere to go. They're all confused. They even swim towards the big hand.

A soft laugh between a sigh and – they're tickling him, they're making friends, so he won't hurt them.

Suddenly, it's very moist in Bobby's room. His pyjamas feel clammy. She knows he likes her fishes – and her turtles, too, he should have said.

When they went into her room, his mother said he shouldn't disturb them. They're making up. And don't you get naughty now, she added. She didn't like the fish-talk at dinner.

It's a cool spring night, but Bobby feels warm, too warm. It's late, but he wants to have a bath, even if she didn't have one, even if the tub won't smell of lavender.

He tiptoes to the bathroom, stopping awhile outside her door. So quiet –

The bath is dry, very dry, but she's wet on the face. She's hugging the creatures to her, lest they stray where there is no water. Under the overbright fluorescent, her sea-dress is only blue and crumpled.

"Auntie . . . ?"

"You're a strange kid," she says without looking at him. She just sits in the bath, rocking the creatures as if sending them to sleep.

"You okay, Auntie . . . ?"

"Auntie's good now, you know. She'll get rid of what gets in the way, so it could be okay again, you understand?"

"The fishes and turtles . . ."

She half-laughs. "All creatures nice and small, yes . . . away with them . . ."

He kneels beside the bath. He wants to tell her not to cry so, to ask why she doesn't turn on the tap.

"You almost understand . . . don't you, Bobby?" She hugs him tightly, her tears hot on his shoulders.

He's drowning in her sea-dress. His throat is dry. Between his legs, there is a strange tightening. He needs to run to the toilet, he doesn't know why, but can't find the strength to leave this big embrace. He wants her to hug him tighter against her fishes and turtles, so they could swim to him, too, and trail this tickle up and down his inner thighs.

# JAR

Tomorrow, I get sacked. The jar and I understand what this means, and what then needs to be done. And done quickly. I remove my coat. I glance at the clock. Eleven. I take a good look at the jar. It is my favourite in this antique shop. I polish it every day.

My boss is at the counter sales-talking an old man. As I amble past them, my boss glares at me. Late again! Bet you, his Adam's apple will strain to escape from his neck after that customer leaves.

But I will explain to him calmly. I have taken up belly-dancing, so I've been late for work for three consecutive days now. He will curse and spit, of course, but I will lead him close to this cupboard where the jar is kept. Here, I will tell him my story.

My belly-dancing went beyond its usual time, I'll say and heave the jar down, then place it between us like a testimony of my admission. I will begin polishing it.

It is made of red earth. An unusually rich red. My boss

once said that I have a jar fixation. But what does he know? He's busy gesticulating now, mesmerising the customer with the play of his short arms. Their encounter will take a long time yet. The boss loves a captured audience, especially one who pays after the show. But I can wait. I must not take the jar down from its cupboard, not yet, though it's raring to be rubbed, polished. Later, when he's here.

I can almost hear him though. "You're at your stupid task again!"

But I will only rub the redness more. "This is my first job of the day. The best piece in your collection must look perfect."

"What's the point in giving excuses, when tomorrow is your last day?"

"It is not an excuse. I've taken up belly-dancing – and I thought it might interest you."

I will alternately rub the jar and my stomach while I tell him about the rudiments of belly-dancing. After a while, his cursing will simmer down to heavy breathing.

"One last time?" he will ask while following my movements with his eyes, then with his hand. I will have to peel off his fingers from my belly.

"It is growing." I can make my voice sound tragic or distraught or elated.

His hand will drop. Panic will leap out of his eyes to smother the part of my anatomy in question.

"You were not careful?" He will shred the room with gestures.

But look at him now, gathering his waving arms back to himself, now that the client has decided on an item. How almost sedate a composure. Later though, I will pity him in his need to piss in his pants. He is a respectable man extremely afraid of his wife. He was in fact shaking the first time he tackled me in the back-room, all along hinting about a raise, and, in the same breath, reminding me about how difficult it is to find a steady job in this time of recession. He knew that, when I came to work for him two months ago, I was a casualty of the nearby restaurant that just went broke.

"How could you be so stupid? I told you to be careful."

He will take the jar from me and return it to its cupboard. He will rearrange the displays. It is his habit to order things in the shop when he contemplates the difficulties of his world. But now he is busy contemplating profit instead as he wards off all bargaining at the counter. They're taking a long time. Suits me though. I can rehearse my answers when he starts with his queries.

"What do we do now?"

"I'm sure you have nothing against my belly-dancing."

"You're punishing me? If it's because of tomorrow, I tell you, there's nothing much that you or I can do. The wife . . . oh, God, help us."

The other day, two weeks after he met the new girl in the fish and chips shop next door, I figured he had offered her my salary with a bonus to boot. He had a long heart-to-heart with her across the counter. He commiserated with her low wages, all along rubbing her arm. Then he took me aside to say that his wife was getting suspicious, so, much to his disappointment, I really must go. After that customer leaves, he will reiterate his fears.

"She can make it very difficult for you. For us. You should have been careful. You should have – you must do something. You must."

"I'm doing something. I'm telling a story."

"Stop mocking me."

"My dancing caused it to grow."

"Will you stop – ?"

"Even my navel is growing."

"All your idiotic –"

"It's growing a mouth, a black mouth – you don't understand my story, do you?"

"This is a trick."

I will try to hold back the laughter in my belly.

"You're not – you're only pulling my leg?"

But it will spill through my skin, through my fingers.

"Tell me you're only joking."

My laughter will spill all over the floor, and rise up, up –

"I'm only joking?"

To the cupboard where the jar is kept.

"You don't really mean it."

It will fill the jar.

"Of course, I don't really mean it."

"So what was all that? A last try for the back-room?"

I see he's relieved now. The old man has stopped haggling. But he's not about to let him go. He wants to schmooze him up some more, in case a second sale could be arranged. I figure he is the first and only customer this morning. No, I cannot wait. I will start with the jar now. It has a part in my story. I must not forget to explain this to him.

"Wait. Don't you want to know why my belly's growing a black mouth?"

"You can be funny sometimes – and I love it. Oh, will I miss you."

"This jar did it. You know I polish it every day. Well, last week, while I was giving it a final rub, it just spoke – imagine, it spoke, and recommended belly-dancing. So I signed up for a class. That was the time when my navel began to grow a mouth."

"Naughty belly button."

"And it promised to grow teeth."

"You can always come and visit, y'know."

The cooing sounds in his throat will make me want to pat his little bulge with the impatient understanding one reserves for a fickle child.

"But, maybe, we can postpone your leaving, hey?"

In the back-room he will lay me on the usual antique table with the exotic carvings on its surface. For many afternoons, I had left work with flowers on my back.

There is some hearty backslapping going on at the counter now. Another sale, it seems. The old man is beaming while the clever salesman hands him his card, just in case – but where was I? Oh, yes. As I said, I will be on the table and under heavy breathing in the back-room.

"Now let's see you demonstrate what you've learned in that belly-dancing class of yours."

He will probe my navel with his little finger in his version of foreplay. I forgot to say he goes crazy over belly buttons. He cannot proceed without measuring their depth with his little finger.

"Ouch! So it bites." He will play the game from where he cannot withdraw.

His little finger will get stuck. My navel-teeth shall see to that. Then the finger beside his little finger will also get stuck, sucked in like the third finger. Then the hand, the arm, the shoulder, the screaming head, the struggling upper torso, then the pelvis that will have lost what little bulge it had, down to the kicking bony legs and feet, all will be swallowed up. He will disappear.

In the evening his frantic wife will phone me. I will say he must have gone to the bar as I flush the last remnants of what, I suppose, will upset my stomach.

I'm rubbing it now, by the way, as I polish this jar. Good jar. Good belly.

From the counter, the little man is yelling. "Pick up your feet and attend to the phone!"

Thank God, finally, he let his captive go. I give the jar, then my belly, another good rub. He hurls an expletive in my direction. It bounces on me, bounces on the jar and disintegrates in mid-air. He answers the phone himself. I walk towards him with my hand still on my stomach rehearsing its dance story. My navel-teeth graze my fingers to remind me this is not fiction.

# FLORES DE MAYO

When the one and only bus that comes to our village announces itself like the song of crickets and the house is too heavy with *siesta*, my feet begin to itch for the much-delayed flower hunt. I take out my white paper basket and watch my toes wiggle impatiently. In her half-sleep, Grandmother mumbles that I should not forget my slippers. But how do I climb the *kanda* in slippers? Or wade the marsh for the fragrant *kamya*? Or when I get really desperate, scour the rice paddies for the occasional white *bandera española*? You see, Grandmother, if Mother were here, she would have understood that white flowers become impossibly rare in May. I have to be on my bare toes all the time, I want to remonstrate. But I hear the musical drone of her dream-breath again, so I tiptoe through the door instead, still in my bare feet.

Outside, the bus has lost its magic. My friend Pilar, who is just now painfully squeezing out of its cramped belly, laughs at me every time I tell her about its cricket-song. The rusty tin can groans, she says, adding, but how would you know when you rarely go to town? So I retort, and how would you know when you're hardly ever out of its belly and listening, *aber*? The bus is one of our pet arguments. We have a good many of them, perhaps because I'm a village girl and she, a town girl. Unlike her, I hate wearing slippers or shoes. How can anyone be so stupid as to race or catch dragonflies in them anyway? I tell Pilar to stop acting like a grandmother, or her hair will grow white and her teeth will fall out one by one. She's a funny girl, this Pilar. She scares easily, so she heeds my advice, then we become friends again. But we're never real enemies, you know. She's Grandmother's *ejada* or goddaughter, which makes her my god-someone-or-other. Grandmother explains this web of affinity every now and then, especially when I fight Pilar, but it's too complicated to repeat. Besides, I sense another fight brewing, so I can forget it. She was supposed to come this morning.

To think that she must stay in our house for the night! It's the last day of the *Flores de Mayo* and there will be a big celebration at church late this afternoon, so she must miss the last bus back to town. In case you don't know, the *Flores* is a church thing for us young girls. It runs for the whole month of May. Now imagine all of us hunting for white flowers, and I mean really white, to offer to the Blessed Virgin. I don't mind the hunt. I actually enjoy it, except when there's too much competition, and especially when I can't start on time. The roses and the gardenias go either to those with gardens at home or to the early and best beggars from those with gardens at home. But persuasion is a waste of time with stingy neighbours. It's easier to wait till their backs are turned. But, oh, how can you steal for the Virgin? Pilar is always horrified. Precisely. I can steal if it is for the Virgin,

I say. Oh, then you must confess, the silly girl insists. Why should I, when she knows it already – it's my turn to laugh at her.

Here in Iraya, we laugh a lot, especially in May when the ricefields have become more gold than green, and everywhere flowers are bursting into all colours, except white. You find the white in church at four o'clock in the afternoon, when we line up in our white smocks, shoes and socks, with our frilled white paper baskets which hold our all-white booty for the Virgin. Sometimes I wonder if she ever gets bored at our lack of imagination as we litter her aisle with petals and petals of only white. We do not really throw them on the floor, mind you. I'm still trying to master how to cast them down with just the right flick of the wrist as we march towards the altar in pairs, singing the "*Dulcissima Virgen*". Sometimes, it bothers me that her ears might hurt when our high notes lurch off their peak. So when I see my music teacher squirm from the front pew, I swallow my voice and mouth the words instead, as I prop up the stray notes in my head. They're always in place in here, and almost beautiful. Maybe, if we all stayed quiet, we might hear them from their precarious height. As always, Pilar finds my theory silly. But look who's sillier now? The *Flores* won't be till later, but she's all dressed up already.

"You took a long time." I notice the beautiful silk ribbon around her waist.

"Look, Connie. Look what the driver did to my hem. He burned it with his cigarette."

"You're very late." She has a new pair of shoes as well.

"Can't you see how bad it is?"

"I don't care. I've been waiting for you since this morning."

"You think Mother will spank me when she sees this?"

"I don't care. I don't live with a mother." Her socks have lace on them, too.

"Oh, what an awful man, that driver."

"I don't care." And she has roses in her basket?

"Is that all you can say?"

"I don't care." How dare she have roses in her basket!

"You're just jealous, because my dress is new. I'll go and ask *Ninang* to fix it." She rushes to the house, calling for Grandmother.

"I don't care!" I shout at her, then stare at my empty basket. I don't mind her new dress or new shoes, or her socks with lace on them, but she has roses. Imagine, roses! And yesterday, she promised she would come early to hunt flowers with me. Of all things, roses! She's showing off.

"Consuelo, come up here! What have you done to Pilar again, ha?"

"I can't, Grandmother. I'm off to find flowers."

"Consueloooo!"

Grandmother says I was not rightfully named. That I am not her *consuelo* – not her joy or consolation, but her despair. Like my mother. But I'm not a bad girl, believe me. And I don't think Mother is all that bad either. She's just too busy to visit. Besides, there are many reasons for goodness other than Grandmother's reasons or Pilar's or the neighbours'. Right now, mine is more than good. I can't waste my time with Pilar's hem, because I can't do anything about it anyway. Grandmother's voice grows fainter and fainter as I rush off to my holy mission.

I pass the bald *kanda* tree of Tiya Bising, our next-door and only generous neighbour. Someone has been there before me. My empty basket suddenly feels heavy. I dig my toes into the earth, and make believe they're bugs burrowing, or roots. I pretend I'm becoming a tree and I don't have to go to the *Flores*. I can't walk. I can't hunt flowers. Look, I stretch my limbs into branches, and my hair turns green. My best friend and god-someone-or-other has cheated on me, and comes with roses. And my grandmother loves her more. And I have a mother, but she rarely visits. I am a tree.

"Hoy, Connie, have you turned into stone?" Tiya Bising is laughing from her window. I sometimes feel there's too much laughter in May.

"I am a tree."

"So the spirits are up to their tricks again with you, ha?"

"I am a tree."

"Come up here, you funny girl, and have some of my *leche flan*."

I'm shameless when it comes to food, especially sweet things. I don't need a second invitation. Tiya Bising's *leche flan* is the best egg custard in the village. And she's our prettiest old woman, next to Grandmother. This afternoon, she wears her tortoiseshell comb with glitter and her sequined shoes, and she smells of caramel. She tells me she had planned to go to town, but that she had missed the bus which brought Pilar. Between mouthfuls, I tell her about Pilar and her new dress, new shoes and socks with lace on them, and her roses, of course. I emphasise the roses. And I advise her to listen hard to the cricketsong of the bus next time, so she won't miss it. She looks at me strangely and laughs again, saying I have funny ideas. Why is everyone like Pilar today?

"So your basket is empty." Tiya Bising smooths its ragged paper frills.

I'm not good at curling paper with the scissors' edge, so the frills around the bottom of the basket can bounce-dangle charmingly. Cut one side of the paper into strips and curl each one of them with the sharp edge of the scissors. That's how all of us girls are supposed to do it. Everyone can, except me. I wish I were a regular girl. I lick my spoon.

"You should have come this morning. I gave all my *kanda* flowers to the Garcia girls."

What can you expect? Five girls can demolish a tree. I tell Tiya Bising not to worry, because I'll find something. I blame Pilar for being late, and excuse myself. I need to be in business or the Virgin will have one basket less of white flowers. Tiya Bising understands. She doesn't mind me running off after the feast at her table. Eat-and-run, as we say. She knows too well that I'm a busy girl today.

I head for the marsh, walking through a swarm of dragonflies. Giants and dwarfs, and needle-thin ones which we call *dagom-dagom*. I think they are baby dragonflies. I stand very still in their midst. I even stop breathing. I do this trick often with them. It always works, like now. A pair, one giant deep blue, the other needle-thin and slightly blue, alight on each of my shoulders. Mother and daughter, I suppose. I glance at them from the corner of my eye. They're curious about this flowerless girl. I hold my breath longer, too long, I feel my chest might burst open, and my heart might jump out and join them. As if comprehending, the mother blue takes off and lands on my chest. It's listening to my heart. It hears about Pilar and Grandmother and Mother and Tiya Bising and her *leche flan*, and the cricketsong no one believes in. I wonder how its tiny body can hold all the stories of my day. I sneeze. The baby one flew too close to my nose. The pair flies off. I leap onto a stone and descend into the marsh.

Nothing. Some clever girl raided my secret flower kingdom. All the *kamya* are gone. Perhaps because it's the last day of the *Flores*, and everyone is desperate to have a basket brimming with white. I run my basket over the headless stalks. The mosquitos wake and hum their sympathy. I clap one dead as it gets too friendly on my ear, but the sudden movement makes me slip – the basket flies from my hand and gets caught in a *milflores* bush at the other bank as I land waist-deep-smack on the mud! A king-frog surveys his visitor through half-lidded eyes, croaks twice, and hops away. In frogspeak, it must mean, "Naughty! Naughty!" Almost like Grandmotherspeak.

"It would have been worse if I had my slippers on." I argue with the retreating frog, the headless stalks, the mosquitos, the mud, and the *milflores* on the bank as I haul myself out of the marsh. My surprisingly still immaculate-white basket flutters its limp frills in a slight breeze, as if to remind me we are on opposite banks, and that I'll have to cross the muddy water to retrieve it. It had chosen to catch its handle on a branch drooping with the weight of lilac clusters. *Milflores*, thousands of flowers – but they are not white. My basket quivers proudly in the wind though. Perhaps, it thinks itself aptly positioned. Lilac and white. Look at me, it seems to say. I have some colour now, some contrast, unlike you stupid girls who are uninterestingly pale every afternoon in your bloodless frocks.

I am suddenly caught with a crazed inspiration. I wade to the other side, rescue my basket, and pick a bunch of *milflores*. As I wade back, I chance upon a stalk of fire-red *bandera española*. I pluck it, too, staining my fingers with its sap. Then I clamber up to safety, where some wild *cadena de amor* creep in profusion. I twine a crown from its vines around my head, and prance about, gathering a handful of the tiny pink buds. The scheme in my mind is as colourful as the prize in my basket. I feel quite heady. I pull up tufts of grass as well as I walk home. The swarm of dragonflies buzzes around me. *Chismosas*, I hush them conspiratorially. Spying gossips! They don't leave me alone until I climb over our back fence.

It's nearly four o'clock now and Grandmother must be waiting with her *tumagiktik*, the dried bamboo rod, ready for my wayward bum. I dare not walk through the front gate with the state of my unshod feet and, worse, my mudcaked limbs. I wonder where Pilar is. I sneak through the cacao and coffee shrubs. I nearly stumble over Karing, our pregnant sow, as I rush to the well among the guava trees. I quickly draw some water and strip down to my underpants. Grandmother says the well spirits always keep watch from below, so one must never bathe completely naked. They can blow air into your vagina and you might bloat like Karing. I wonder whether Mother ever bathed naked near a well. The last time she visited, her tummy looked strange. She seldom visits, because she's too busy, she said. Grandmother harrumphed and drew her lips into a thin line when Mother explained this to me. I asked her then, what keeps you busy? Dancing, she answered and stopped short when Grandmother snapped at her. Mother gave me a quick hug and left in a rush. I remember her tummy looked strange. I must not forget to ask her the next time she comes whether there's a well near the place where she dances. I must warn her about the spirits.

Mother dances in Manila, where there are bright lights, she said – Manila is a very big city with too many buses. Imagine how loud their cricketsong must be. But Mother said there are no crickets in the big city. I hope she does not miss the bus to her dance then. Being late for it is as bad as being late for my *Flores* now. I really must hurry. I give my feet a final douse of water, while vigorously rubbing them together to get rid of the mud, roll my dress into a small ball, pick up my basket, and hurriedly sneak through the kitchen door. I wonder where Pilar is.

I hear a familiar voice from the bedroom. Tiya Bising!

Just my luck. Grandmother never whacks me when there's a visitor. I pat my wet wayward bottom confidently and walk into the room, dripping and wearing my most engaging smile.

"Grandmother, I'm all washed and ready, see?"

Everyone stares at me from the bed. Pilar is as pale as her white dress. Tiya Bising has her arms around Grandmother. She's making funny noises, there's a steady stream on her cheeks. I've never seen her like this before. I get scared and confused. I drop my ball of clothes and the basket of flowers. The puddle around me becomes bright with petals. I don't know why, but I begin to cry. Maybe I hurt Grandmother, because I ignored her call a while back. Maybe she's so angry, she'll whip my skin off.

"I didn't mean to, Grandmother. I'm sorry for running off. I'm sorry, too, for not wearing my slippers."

A twig snaps in Grandmother's throat. She hugs me tightly, I can't breathe. Tiya Bising turns away to hide her face. Pilar wails on her white skirt.

"And I was going to play a trick on the Virgin, Grandmother. I was going to the *Flores* with flowers not white."

Grandmother trembles at hearing my latest prank. She can't stop shaking and making more strange sounds in her throat. "Something happened, Connie – your mother –"

"A bus did it, Connie. Ay, a very big bus. Bigger than our bus." Pilar is sobbing like a cow, I can't hear Grandmother clearly.

She cups my face with both her shaking palms and looks at me with the saddest, gentlest eyes. "Connie, dear, your mother – she's coming home –"

"Is that why you're upset, Grandmother?"

"Connie, dear –"

"You don't want her here?"

"Connie –"

"Why are you always angry with her?"

She keeps on crying out my name as if I were far away, and she were calling me back. I push her away.

"Is her tummy all right?"

# SPLINTER

This is my salvation, this sliver in my palm. You suck it out and we both come. Before this train gets to Central, let me tell you, it can happen. It's probably festering, see? Here, right here at the centre of my palm, where the lifeline crosses the heartline.

You don't believe me? Take a close look then. That hardly discernible dot like a nudge from a fine point pen, that's the tip of the thing. You doubt it? Feel it then, the way you'd search for an invisible, fucking splinter that gets stuck in your skin when you clean up a mess. A pinpoint ache that seems not to be there, but insists it is whenever you accidentally rub the skin. Almost like a pretend affliction, because it seems so inconsequential, but hurts anyway.

You beautiful boy, don't you understand? My palm is sending messages to your mouth, to your half-opened lips made for sucking. You yawn, I shiver slightly over those strong, even teeth which could bite the tip of this shard and pull it out, both of us sighing afterwards, as if blessed even before arriving at the terminal. For this is every heart's desire on a Friday rush hour, all of us throwing our bodies into train carriages, crying save me, save me. There is a pinpoint ache somewhere, show me where, and, please, kiss it better.

Me? I know where it is. You don't have to find it for me. I am certain. Suck my palm. You Catholic? Heard about one of the wounds of Christ? It doesn't matter. I'm lapsed anyway, religious shelf life over when I left my country – what about you? You ethnic, too – once? No worries, I'm as Aussie as you now. I love steak and onion pie, by the way, with lots of chilli sauce, an old habit. Makes lips burn, oh-oh.

I love your lips, beautiful boy. I love Australia. I love you to suck my palm.

Palm sex. Rings a bell, I know, what with the joke about Mrs Palmer and her five lovely daughters. Wish I could find that funny, but like the act it's too obvious and predictable. Fondle-rub-oooh-fondle-rub-rub-hah-hah-hah-hah-ooooooooh God! And you're not even Catholic.

But palm sex is something else. It's the act of any stranger sucking the centre of your palm, where the lifeline and heartline intersect, to draw out the nasty ache hiding there. A thorn or sliver of glass or wood or the thinnest chip of china from the last decent plate in the house after one of its creatures had lost her temper.

I think it was the Wedgwood cake plate which she hurled at me, minus the cake, but missed. I swear I saw a white Attic nose jumping out before the crash, wanting to be saved like me. Half past twelve when I ran out the door, hugging myself for dear life. Just in time before her china armoury was depleted, yeah, yeah.

You keep looking at your watch, that ticking wound on

your wrist which infuriates me. I'm jealous of your many appointments, the way you wear them as if your life depended on them. I ditched mine, you know, fifteen minutes ago at the ticket counter. There was a long, motionless queue as some wog pestered the ticket man for directions. Well, I was a wog once, I pestered ticket men for directions once, but I'm better now. Once a wog, always a wog, I don't believe that, you see.

I have ditched time, ditched history, I mean, ditched my watch at the ticket counter with its fucking slow-mo queue. I actually tried to crush it in my hands for good measure, then finished it off with a good grind of the heel. After being attacked by a flying Wedgwood cake plate, the last thing I needed was an extreme reversal of pace. I was going to miss this train, I was going to miss you, to miss me with you, because of that bloody slow queue and – you know what – my hurrying bloody Seiko. Let me tell you, its hands must have been afflicted by the speed of the flying Wedgwood plate or by my pulse outrunning the speed of its flight. The fucking Seiko had doubled up its speed – tickitickitickitick instead of tick-tick-tick-tick.

Don't do that – I can't think straight every time you catch me with the corner of your half-lidded eye – no, yes, do that all over again, ooooh, yes, then suck my palm. Suck it out, please, this hint of white from the thinnest chip of china or this splinter of Seiko time, whichever, suck out my story, my history, and let us come then, you and I. Where the sigh is sweet like a fart etherising the goddamn bed, smart ass. My boy, a lot of people fart after sex, do you know that?

But palm sex is better than sex sex, result hundred per cent guaranteed. We both come or your money, no, your precious time back. How to do it? Turn it back, of course, pretend it never happened, fuck history, simple. And when we get to

Central, we would have forgotten that you serviced my hand, that we caught each other's eye, that we sat opposite each other or that we even took this train.

You have the habit of giving back, giving up time! She had screamed before launching the Wedgwood missile. She was, of course, referring to the act of relinquishing past time, my abandoning our history. That silly cow and her quaint English, never qualifies her statements – giving up time? What do you mean, you idiot! The crux of her aggro was the fact that I usually forget things.

Ah, more soma versus history, that's what the world needs, I reckon. That's what will save us to enjoy a moment like this, darling. Fuck history and ditch its making. Palm sex with no responsibility at all, babe. No pills, no condoms, no pregnancies, low AIDS risk, or none at all, no worries about the little lover waiting back home, no angst over the memories of ex-fucks. All in a train's ride, hey, quicker than the quickest quickie if you know where to suck. You'll know, because I'll tell you. Here, see here, where the lifeline and the heartline intersect. And you don't even have to be a palm reader.

She is though, my general of the crockery, my weird Mama is. Weeps into my hands, as if reading my palms, when she gets a wee tipsy – "Oh, my black sheep child's memory is shorter than her miniskirt, sweet Jesus. She goes to church no more, prays no more, eats my cooking no more, too much fish and chips and booze, will come home no more." Imagine, the silly cow wants us to fly back to her hovel over there. There – where? Must visit my sisters there, she says, so I can tell them about my Wedgwood collection here in Australia. Minus the cake plate, of course.

Finally you're beginning to smile at me, to half-smile. You have caught my fever, oh, yeah – but you've been quite slow, haven't you? Why don't you come over, sit beside me, as if there were only us in this carriage, baby, you and me against the railway line, and I'll show you where the splinter is, then you'll swoon in the joys of sucking. Don't you know that palms itch when you're horny? That's why a knowing lover scratches them when he wants some.

What, you fancy the view outside more than me? Hey, look again, I've got excellent credentials, darling. I'm not just any girl, you know, I'm at Uni now – surprise, surprise. Yeah, a long shot from the lot of my poor Mama. She's proud of me, of course, even if she weeps over my short skirts and booze – sure, I'm not just any girl. I've scrubbed off my wog-ness with HDs, let me tell you. Had to explain this to her. High Distinction, the highest possible mark at University, Mother, meaning, I'm top of my class. HD! She thought it sounded like some dirty disease that they talk about on TV. I nearly pissed myself laughing. Hey, silly, this means you're now facing a brilliant girl –

But still you won't look at me – hey, I may work my arse off at school, but I do know how to let my hair down, like my knickers, yes, down to my knees, especially now that I've got a verrrry hot palm – c'mon, take its temperature – but oh you're shy, you won't even budge from your seat. Is it more comfortable there? Well, let me find out.

You shift your bum to give way to mine, hey, gentleman beauty? Uhmm . . . I love your heat, shoots straight to the cunt, bull's-eye, then zooms to the palm, like an electric shock, whew! Feel it – hey, I could lay me on your thigh, what about that? Much better than a begging bowl, huh? Yeah, bare palms are sexier, like this, outstretched. The pass-ing donor can read lifelines, heartlines, the brevity of exis-tence, and his power to extend it with that extra centavo, of course –

"The train on platform eleven goes to Sutherland . . ."

C'mon, don't be such a killjoy, mister train – you want me to go back, to re-track me, before I have even started my joy ride, hey? Bad luck for us, dearest, Central Station now, but must we go? Let's ride back, yes, let's, to the finish. This is our salvation, this sliver in my palm. You suck it out and we both come. Before this train gets to Sutherland, let me tell you, it will happen – hey, hey, wait, I'll get off with you, of course –"

". . . *et demie* . . ." her voice trails away.

Fuckkkk! Whatta kiss, man, ooooh – did I see that? So you like her better, huh? A pro-active Frog instead of a beggar girl like me, hey, you hear me? What, me blocking the door, of course not, sir, just get in, hop in, ma'am, and don't mind me standing here, just ogling my aborted boyfriend while he paws another girl, shit!

"The train on platform eleven goes to . . ."

". . . *déjeuner* . . . ?"

"*Oui, oui . . . mon cheri . . .*"

Wogs! Of course, both of you genuine wogs. Stupid me, I should have sniffed out your secret, my dreamboat wog – but what about my palm, hey, babyyyy –?

". . . all doors closing . . ."

Huuups! Nearly got my coat there, damn door – well, what are you staring at, huh? Huh? Something the matter? I'm a good Aussie citizen just having a bad day, so what's new? Why, you want to see my palm, too, you mister, you, ma'am, oh, keep your eyes to yourselves, will you?

". . . First stop, Hurstville . . ."

Aw, stop wherever you want. Take me back home, yeah, but bloody shut up! Turn the journey upside down, turn the point of origin into one fucking destination, who cares? Yeah, send me home to a Wedgwood-throwing Mama while the

Frogs seek their own croak on a horny p.m. and the wheel of fortune rolls back – fuck this palm. History hurts!

# THE WIND WITCH

| | |
|---|---|
| 1. Girl with windmill | forever |
| 2. Woman with tiny bottle | perfume |
| 3. Mother and crying baby with cassette recorder | lullaby |
| 4. Man with oxygen tank | muscle |
| 5. Boy with sail | horizon |
| 6. Chef with spice shaker | aroma |
| 7. Grandmother with snuffbox | rest |
| 8. Woman with empty hands | confidential |
| 9. Man with nothing on | confidential |

10, 11, 12, etc., etc., . . . It was a long list with a long journey back, as it was passed from hand to hand from the end of the queue, which was now at the entrance of Kings Cross train station, until it got back to the girl with the windmill and was finally handed over to the hands waiting inside the blue, cotton tent in front of St John's Church in Darlinghurst. A long queue indeed, and it was still lengthening, so the inhabitant of the tent wisely abandoned further listings, at least for the moment, and decided to commence the business which everyone had "enlisted" for.

All would have a chance, such was the assurance from the tent. Thus the tedious operation, of each newly arrived petitioner filling out the list and passing it on to the next person, was shelved for an hour or so.

The street was in chaos, traffic was blocked, curious drivers and pedestrians had stopped and forgotten where they were going, coffee shops were packed with even more curious clients who decided to have multiple cups of coffee until the action began, and the yet curiouser police gaped like everyone else, refusing to break this procession of petitioners. Chaos, yes, but benevolent chaos. Elbows were not as sharp, bodies leaned against one another and generously allowed others to squeeze in, cars did the same, no one honked, voices played a range of timbres, from curious-doubtful to curious-awed, all primed with excitement, but not quite agitated or impatient, even if it was a very hot day. Thirty-six degrees and windless, almost everyone thought so, at least.

"Number One, please."

Nothing special about the announcement from the tent. It sounded more like a call in a take-away joint, with the same tone and attitude that told you, your order is ready, come and get it, yes, that drone that you only half-listened to – but not this time. All ears were straining to capture the weight of each word, syllable, vowel, consonant, for it must have more weight than it sounds, shouldn't it, especially on this occasion.

"It's a she—it's a she—it's a she—" The crowd's first discovery about the tent's inhabitant, upon clearly hearing her voice, rippled the air so quickly, that, as it travelled the street, it sounded more like a hush, an urgent demand for silence which was instantly heeded.

The girl with the toy windmill stretched herself and shuffled her shoes, as if she were bracing herself for a race, clutched her toy even tighter, breathed in, and walked into the tent.

Rebecca, that was her name, heard about it last night, the only night when she forgot to close her window before going to bed. Maybe that was why she found out, though she never actually saw the source of the advertisement which was blown into her dreams:

WIND-WISH, WIND-GIFT! YOUR HEART'S DESIRE BY AIR. BRING A BOTTLE. 8:00 A.M., ST JOHN'S CHURCH, VICTORIA STREET, DARLINGHURST.

A funnel of wind, from some source that blurred in her dream, wrote out the ad, disappeared, then rushed back to complete it with a P.S. BOTTLE NOT COMPULSORY. ANY RECEPTACLE WILL DO. And, of course, there was also the fine print which she did not bother to read.

Eight-year-old Rebecca brought her toy windmill and her heart's desire. Ever after. That conclusion of all the fairytales that her parents had read to her. Ever after – yet the story always ended, its reading was always finished, her parents always closed the book afterwards, kissed her goodnight and turned off the lamp. Forever? She wanted it real, she wanted proof, perhaps in the endless turning of her toy windmill beside the lamp. She wanted nothing less than infinity to grace her bedside table.

It was a surprised kind of laughter, like short exclamations and queries combined – "Ha!-ha?-ha!" – followed by similarly toned bursts of air – "Prrp!-prrp?-prrp!" – insistent plosives that seemed to rev, but in a delicate way, a miniature fugue which teased the crowd into pronouncing a host of speculations. Eventually, most concluded that it was, of course, a very brief conversation between the girl with the windmill – and SHE! By now, everyone had begun thinking of the inhabitant of the tent in terms of capital letters.

Emerging, as if from a blue veil, the windmill would not stop turning like its laughing bearer who whirled through the astonished crowd – what's with her and what's with HER? – as if in a frenzied waltz up Victoria Road, past more coffee shops, past St Vincent's Hospital, and all the way to Oxford Street.

"Number Two, please."

The tiny bottle was straightforward; the woman was, too, though there was something ambivalent about her lips. One end tilted upwards, the other down, as if she couldn't quite decide whether she'd smile or cry or, perhaps, pout, who knows. She was wearing a yellow slip and mauve sandals. Her lips were mauve as well. Around her eyes, well, a greenish-yellow-mauve eye-shadow that reminded one of a fruit's various stages of ripening. Marina was unhappily in between these stages, so when the fan at her writing desk whirred her the ad about wind-wishes and all, just as she was about to drift off to a *siesta*, she was instantly inspired to bring her own bottle.

Marina longed for the perfume of words. And each scent has to be precise, she thought, so that it can never be mistaken for another. Word: Scent: Source. Marina argued in these terms. A true word should be like perfume; the bottled fragrance must instantaneously conjure the actual flower. And if you had the true word for everything in life, then you could write. And all your readers' noses would be inevitably enticed, become preoccupied, hopelessly engaged and challenged, even embattled as they were led through a maze and into a smelly truth that is like no other.

"Number Two – ?"

"Coming, coming," Marina muttered to herself as she lifted the flap of the tent.

It grew very still and silent, a condition which contaminated the length of the street. Even breathing was arrested, until the blue cotton began to billow, as if, on that still summer's day, a gust of wind had erupted from the pavement, but only at this chosen spot.

"Gardenias."

"No, mildew."

"Apples!"

"Wrong, sweat!"

"Oh, sweet basil . . ."

"Apricots, yes, yes."

"Mother's tears!"

"Fish entrails?"

"I think, jackfruit . . ."

"My God, corpses!"

As the billowing began to subside, noses were seized, entranced, assaulted by the smells of everyone's dream, despair, desire, damnation, but only very briefly, because the olfactory feast ended when Marina emerged, triumphant with all these conjured scents bottled at last. She looked around, bowed gracefully towards the crowd, practising how great writers might do it, and slipped the gift into her pocket.

Not comprehending the full meaning of the two successful miracles, but seeing the almost beatific delight on the faces of Numbers One and Two, most of the audience came to a personal decision – passers-by, drivers, coffee-drinkers, gawkers, even a policeman, searched themselves for anything that could contain wind, perhaps a plastic bag, an empty bottle of wine, an electric fan, a balloon and, heavens, even a condom, any possible dream-receptacle, as they jostled each other towards the queue which was now crawling towards the far end of Potts Point.

"Number Three?"

A dance with its own accompaniment. The mother swaying, jigging and humming to hush her crying son. Petra and little Pietro intimately performing together one of the oldest shows in the world. The longest running production they'd ever had, for neither had slept for three days now, because Pietro was extending his tantrum and poor Petra had just exhausted all means, both medical and mythical, to contain her baby's anguish. So when she saw the writing on the wall behind the stove – the beef goulash had steamed the ad there – she scoured her fogged mind for the best medium that would do justice to a gift of the wind. Breath. Notated breath. Song. Lullaby! And what better thing to contain it than a cassette recorder.

Number Three disappeared into the tent. Those who have not yet enlisted their own desires waited for more reason to join the queue.

"Puuuuu–huuuu-huuuu-huuuu–uuuuuuuuut-t-t-t-t-t-t-t-t-t . . ."

A most liquid, languid violin wail, or was it more like a closed-mouth sigh, with a hint of vibrato at its tail, like the golden curlicue from sleepy and silent little Pietro's nape. Hugging both peaceful baby and playing recorder, Petra walked out of the tent, away from it, and never looked back.

"Number Four now, please . . ."

Anyone would think the man was going diving or, perhaps, had a medical condition that kept him strapped to an aquamarine oxygen tank which matched his lycra singlet and shorts. Excelsior, oh, yes, that was his name, had arrived running at eight sharp and had been running in place since then. It was about ten by this time, and exceedingly humid. In fact, he had already sweated a little pool at his feet, but he grinned at everyone anyway and waved before jogging into the tent. He was fit all right, enough muscles evenly distributed to the right places.

No one knew though that he, indeed, had a condition, and the daily two hour gym work could not alleviate it. It was something about his left bicep and pectoral. They were no doubt packed and sculpted to perfection, but at the end of each day, just before he went to bed, these parts would collapse, sag, behave like a balloon that had lost its air; it seemed as if the core of that left breast was losing its conviction to appear robust at all. This, of course, was enough reason to miss gym today and queue for the wind-gift which was promised by the ad, which had materialised from the fumes of his Porsche when it conked out on his way to a costume party two nights ago, how embarrassing.

"Omigod, is this it – ?" Shock-horror, that was how he sounded to the waiting petitioners and the again growing crowd. While most of the original gawkers began queuing up, including the coffee shop owners themselves, several journos had started to arrive, in dribs and drabs, with their cameras, microphones and little notebooks and, of course, mobile phones. Apparently, someone from the queue had rang someone who also rang someone who believed this "aberrant event", that was how the last someone put it, was big, big NEWS!

"I'm not sure I want – really – ?"

Have you ever heard someone huffing and puffing while reciting an unintelligible nursery rhyme, with all but the consonants disintegrating at the end of each line? Well, that was the response to Excelsior's query, or how the next person in the queue likened it to.

The exquisite percussion generated by the inhabitant of the tent, that was Excelsior's more informed perception, lasted about fifteen minutes, a long wind-transfusion it seemed, well, what with the size of his oxygen tank, so that several people in the queue had begun making impatient noise –

"I love it, it's the greatest – the most ingenious, hilarious – but I'm not giving away anything –" he winked at the boy with the folded sail behind him, while patting his left bicep and breast, bicep and breast, bicep and breast, keeping time with his sprint away from the site of his conversion and, of course, from the journos who were hot on his tail.

Number Five did not need to be called in. Izhiguro, the eight-year-old boy, literally stormed the tent, nearly knocking it down with his eagerness. The journos wanted to rush in as well, but the whole queue booed them and demanded that they wait for their turn –

"Queue up, queue up, queue up, queue up!" The chant was an ejaculatory roar of longing bodies snaking along Darlinghurst, through Kings Cross, to Potts Point and echoing even in Elizabeth Bay.

Longing. Let's keep track of the crux of this occasion, lest we miss the point. Heart's desire + Wind-Gift = Relief, Satisfaction, Satiation, Completion, Culmination, all of the above, all achieved by air, by some wind-magic bestowed by the inhabitant of the blue tent.

Longing. The cops had begun to shift uneasily in a battle between duty – they were supposed to remain indifferent to the action in order to control it – and personal desires. Or was it not their anxiety, which began to surface when the journos started the rounds of interviewing, note-taking, shooting, etc, etc, yes, their anxiety at being adjudged guilty of longing like anyone else on the street and, worse, at having their own longings documented? The police were not used to stating the most intimate details about themselves; they only took statements.

One by one, the men in blue began to behave themselves again, but with much inner struggle, mind you, to detach themselves from this chain of blatant, unadulterated, unashamed display of vulnerability.

"Queue up, queue up, queue up – !" the chant persisted, taking on a tune, as if the streets were composing the testimony of their yearning.

"Whooooooooo? Whooooooooo? Whooooooooo?"

That silenced them. The owl-query, as one radio reporter described it, was actually the noise made by HER peculiar wind-gift for Number Six, the boy with the sail, but everyone took it as a personalised interrogation.

"Who, me?"

"Yes, you!"

"Not me –"

"Then, who?"

The deflecting or denying of any obvious vested interest, in this queuing up to petition for one's heart's desire, quickly travelled through the line of bodies like an electric current short-circuiting, for the queue's conviction had indeed begun to fray, the community of want disintegrating into each individual's awareness that his or her private wiring had been mercilessly exposed, and was now being documented and may end up on evening TV or some cheesy tabloid, God help us.

"Whoooooooooooooooooooooooooooooooooooooooooooooo ooooooooooooooooooooooooooooooooooooooooo?"

The query followed Izhiguro who had just left the tent, his sail suddenly unfurling, blown open by a query, yes, and lifted, yes, oh, yes, raised off the ground, both sail and boy, and blown up, up, full steam ahead in his dream to sail towards the horizon, for that was his wish, remember?

Number 5. Boy with a sail        horizon

That was what he had listed and had been listing daily in the diary which he had kept in his lunch box ever since he learned how to write.

Then the first helicopter arrived, manned by what looked like a SWAT team. Again, someone had rung someone who had rung someone that "we have a situation here" and the police could not contain it – an Asian boy had been abducted by a recalcitrant wind!

Uncertainty settled in. The queue began to break up just as Number Six nervously entered the tent, right foot advancing, left foot retreating, as a camera was trained on him the whole time, closing up on the spice shaker in his hand. On the late news that night, it would appear as incriminating evidence of his unwavering allegiance to "palatory-olfactorisation", that was how Chef Pierre called his motive, his dream-project to trap all possible aromas that would make every mouth of every nationality water – oh, to mix this multitude into the ultimate spice in one bottle!

But in the tent, Chef Pierre was horrified and grievously offended. "No, you won't, heaven forbid!" He came out, waving the spice shaker about, his face a repository of the collective contempt of the world. "Not in this bottle! Never in my cooking – how dare you, you presumptuous stinker?" He screamed at the inhabitant of the blue tent and stomped as far away as possible from the scene of the aborted sacrilege, so he told everyone later when he finally confessed about what really happened inside. "How dare, *mon Dieu* – how dare – !"

"Yes, how dare you –"

"Come here –"

"And cause traffic –"

"And trouble –"

"And distress –"

"And hope –"

And expose it. This was actually what everyone, who had left the queue for fear of being confirmed vulnerable on TV, in the papers, on radio or just in the eyes of the next person, wanted to accuse the inhabitant of the tent, but they were all afraid to expose themselves any further.

So the gift-giving or the wind-gifting, whichever way you saw it, was dutifully intercepted. So everything returned to normal. So the pedestrians and the drivers remembered where they were going and moved on. So the coffee-drinkers went back to their cups and the coffee-makers cranked up their machines again, and the police resumed their jobs, and the SWAT team look-alike rescued the abducted boy at last.

But, sadly, Numbers Seven to Nine never had their day in the tent, although they did have their own day in court, for, yes, she (now diminished to lower case) was prosecuted by all the people who queued up (except the lucky Numbers One to Five, who were granted their wishes before all were enlightened), by the coffee shop proprietors and clients, the oglers, the pedestrians and drivers, by the police and eventually by the state – and all allegations of inciting hope, so she can trespass on everyone's "privatest matters" (for that was how it came to be written), and all punctilious denials that the same matters ever existed were duly documented by responsible journalism, vanguards of our decency, thank God, they saved us from making total asses of ourselves!

But what was the clincher? The hallmark incident that incensed the crowd into condemning her whom they had begun to regard as their blue-veiled fairy godmother, well, for the time being, really – ?

Now, we have to know more about the inhabitant of the tent, shouldn't we, and what actually transpired behind that mantle of secrecy. I must say this would be much more illuminating than dragging through this page the "confidential" matters of the woman with empty hands (Number 8) and the man with nothing on (Number 9), so I leave them to your imagination –

But her – how did she conduct her sessions with the first six petitioners? Why did the girl with the windmill laugh in surprise the moment she entered the tent? Why was Excelsior in shock-horror? And Chef Pierre – why did he embody all the world's contempt even after believing, for a moment, that she could facilitate his "palatory-olfactorisation" project? So who was she? The last question I shall not engage; the state's dossier on her, which was eventually turned over to the national archives, can answer that.

So back to the blue tent and the woman who was only heard but never seen. You probably want a proper denouement with the usual concluding prattle, so I'll give it to you.

Longing might seem to be all gas, full steam ahead, because it is after all a wind in the gut, some kind of air festering in there. Longing rests in the stomach which breaks up the daily nourishment of our wants. It is in our intestines digesting these wants, though not all the time succeeding and often missing the point – which is the true want, the fake want, the want-want – and in our anal passages that is never allowed to betray this excreta of failure in public, this inability to feel content, this sense of never having been fully nourished despite our thorough process of feeding, digesting and eventual elimination of the superfluous or the indigestible. Longing is at gut-level. No, I'm not trivialising the issue by relocating it and thus robbing the heart of its claim to desire – but where were we? Or where should we be? Of course, at the actual locus of the story, the gut of the narrative. The blue tent in Victoria Road, Darlinghurst, Sydney, New South Wales, Australia.

So back to the resolution, the consequence of all these actions that had just been staged.

At twelve noon, after Chef Pierre walked out on his craving, because its fulfilment was too demeaning, Numbers Seven, Eight and Nine still hoped to get into the tent, but the dispersing queue and the sobering, normalising personal interrogations that went on in each desiring heart, that is if we decide to still locate desire in that particular organ, warned all to keep away from the tent until they found out who she really was and what her motives were, until her tricks were made public –

"Who are you? Show yourself! What's the trick? Who are you? Show yourself! What's the trick?" and so on and so on.

It was a different roar this time, like a rugby game cheer in tempo and pitch, but with a different sonority, because it had a sneer in its reverberations. At last, everyone's uncool vulnerabilities of a moment ago, their left-footed affirmations of this or that silly wish or, worse, desperation and, of course, the incredible shame at having admitted that they were all led by the nose by some desire or despair, and finally that utter embarrassment at having been caught out in their privation, were masked by the most respectable sneer.

The tent kept silent, no more wind-noises, but the tension inside was relayed to every spectator's gut. It was as if the inhabitant were struggling towards the most major decision of her life.

The hand that received the list earlier demurely raised the blue flap.

All were hushed.

A very pale – cheek? – the crowd couldn't quite make out what –

And another –

Cheek!

Jesus! A photographer caught the image up close and closer –

It was the palest, smoothest pair of cheeks he had ever seen – and the brownest eye.

Hands flew over eyes or mouths and the most indignant cry of shock-horror ever made in the history of humanity rose up in the air, which began to take on an alien quality as the Wind Witch wiggled her bottom and let out a most resonant fart!

A lingering, wondrous, wind-driven, percussive explosion that no doubt echoed the prrp!-prrp?-prrp! and the gardenias, mildew, apples, sweat, basil, apricots, mother's tears, fish entrails, jackfruit, corpses! and the puuuuu-huuuu-huuuu-huuuu–uuuuuuuuut-t-t-t-t-t-t-t-t-t-t . . . and the huffing and puffing while reciting an unintelligible nursery rhyme, with all but the consonants disintegrating at the end of each line, and the whoooooooooooooooooooooooooooooooooo? and more, all air that can be packaged, bottled and treasured in the receptacle of one's dreams –

But the audience before that palest ass only heard the biggest fart ever and smelled the full foulness of their communal embarrassment!

Well, different versions of that climactic scene were still all over the papers a month after the tedious court hearings which, expectedly, resulted in a compassionate verdict. First, she was not really convicted, but was instead handed over to a psychiatrist, who could fathom the depths of her psyche, and then to a proctologist, who could do the same for her lower regions, and then write about their findings in a proper book. Second, the parliament passed a bill against farting in public, unanimously voted upon, of course, but which was amended the next day. They could not resist this addendum: No one must give anyone the brown eye. Not ever again.

**Merlinda Bobis**, a Filipino-Australian, swears by the joys of the palate and the sensibility. "It is not simply about consumption of food or words, but delight in all their possible evocations—it is, after all, a shame not to do justice to the little pink animal in the mouth." Bobis is the author of four poetry books, four plays and a collection of short stories. She received the Steele Rudd Award (for the Best Collection of Australian Short Stories, 2000) for *White Turtle (The Kissing)*, the Prix Italia (1998), the Australian Writers' Guild Award (1998) and the Ian Reed Radio Drama Prize (1995) for her play *Rita's Lullaby*, and Philippine national literary awards including the Carlos Palanca (1987, 1989) and the Gawad Cultural Centre of the Philippines for her poetry (1990) in English and Filipino. Her *Summer Was A Fast Train Without Terminals* was short-listed for Australia's *The Age* Poetry Book Award (1998). She is currently writing her first novel, *Fish-Hair Woman*, which received the prestigious New South Wales Writers' Fellowship (2000). Bobis is an accomplished performer of her own poetry, embodying text in dance, music and theatre. She teaches creative writing at the University of Wollongong, Australia.

OTHER BOOKS BY MERLINDA BOBIS

*Rituals*

*Ang Lipad ay Awit sa Apat na Hangin / Flight is Song on Four Winds*
    (Bilingual Edition)

*Cantata of the Warrior Woman Daragang Magayon* (Bilingual Edition)

*Summer Was A Fast Train Without Terminals*

*aunt lute books* is a multicultural women's press that has been committed to publishing high quality, culturally diverse literature since 1982. In 1990, the Aunt Lute Foundation was formed as a non-profit corporation to publish and distribute books that reflect the complex truths of women's lives and the possibilities for personal and social change. We seek work that explores the specificities of the very different histories from which we come, and that examines the intersections between the borders we all inhabit.

Please write, phone or e-mail (books@auntlute.com) us if you would like us to send you a free catalog of our other books or if you wish to be on our mailing list for future titles. You may buy books directly from us by phoning in a credit card order or mailing a check with the catalog order form.

Please visit our website at www.auntlute.com.

Aunt Lute Books
P.O.Box 410687
San Francisco, CA 94141
(415)826-1300

This book would not have been possible without the kind contributions of the Aunt Lute Founding Friends:

Anonymous Donor
Anonymous Donor
Rusty Barcelo
Marian Bremer
Marta Drury
Diane Goldstein

Diana Harris
Phoebe Robins Hunter
Diane Mosbacher, M.D., Ph.D.
William Preston, Jr.
Elise Rymer Turner